To Love and To Cherish

Switched at Marriage, Episode 7

Gina Robinson

Gina Robinson
SEATTLE, WASHINGTON

www.ginarobinson.com

Publisher's Note: This is a work of fiction. Names, characters, places, and incidents are a product of the author's imagination. Locales and public names are sometimes used for atmospheric purposes. Any resemblance to actual people, living or dead, or to businesses, companies, events, institutions, or locales is completely coincidental.

Book Layout ©2013 BookDesignTemplates.com
Cover Photos and Design by Jeff Robinson

To Love and To Cherish, Switched at Marriage 7/ Gina Robinson. — 1st ed.
ISBN 978-0692524602

CHAPTER ONE

Kayla
Looking into the eyes of the man you love can be like looking in the mirror. If you're lucky, and he loves you back, it's like gazing into Snow White's mirror and having his eyes tell you you're the fairest of them all.

At the sound of the elevator doors opening, Data barked and danced around excitedly. Which could only mean one thing...

I froze, wrapped compromisingly in Lazer's arms. The world spun in slow motion as I turned and saw Jus standing in the entryway, Data bounding to him as happily as a puppy in a dog food commercial.

Jus held a bouquet of baby-blue and pink you're-having-my-baby balloons so large it looked like the balloons were about to carry him away. I had no idea how he'd wrestled them into the elevator. Or how much ribbing he would have endured because of them. Even the quantity of balloons was boyish and over-the-top happy. Like Jus. It was so like him to show his happiness in a big way.

On his face was a look of utter devastation and shock as he took in the scene before him—me in my robe in Lazer's arms. He paled. Right then, I felt my world cracking, shattering into a million tiny pieces too small to ever be glued back together into any kind of semblance of whole.

The words on my lips to Lazer froze in place. I'd been saying, *I'll always love you...*

To a casual, outside observer, my words, the embrace, the whole scene, looked damning, yes. But what I was about to say wasn't what they would think. It was so totally innocent as to be laughable. The rest of my unfinished sentence made all the difference. But the remainder of my thought had deserted me. I'd always love him for the good friend he was? Maybe that was it. It was something like that.

I wrenched free from him. Actually, wrench was the wrong word. Lazer dropped his arms from around me at the same time so there wasn't much actual wrenching involved.

"Jus!" I took a step toward him, arms outstretched, hoping against hope that he hadn't misunderstood. That he could be talked down from that ledge of assuming the worst. "Are those for me? How sweet!"

His face was set. He was scarily silent and his jaw was ticking beneath all that facial hair. Irrelevantly, I noticed he needed a trim. My world teetered on the brink of destruction. *And I was noticing his personal grooming?*

I took a step closer, trying not to act guilty when I wasn't and flame the fires of betrayal. "You're home early! Did you take the afternoon off?" I tried to put perky and happy into my voice. I think I mostly succeeded in sounding supremely artificial.

I glanced over my shoulder at Lazer. Who was looking at the balloons and me. And the balloons and Jus. Understanding dawning slowly for someone so sharp.

Crap, crap, *crap!*

I pled with my eyes for help. But Lazer stood there stunned. A bachelor in the headlights of domestic happiness being obliterated.

"Lazer just stopped by to drop off your present early. It's something special just for the two of us. For our eyes only. So naturally he didn't want you opening it in public."

Jus was holding my cell phone. *Odd. How did he get that?* I didn't remember losing it. But I'd been so preoccupied with the party I hadn't missed it. I must have left it at Flash. No wonder Lazer had used the buzzer rather than texting me to let him in.

As I took another step toward Jus, my robe slipped open, revealing my sexy lingerie beneath. An outfit meant only for him.

He shot me a disgusted look, so at odds with the way he usually looked at me with love and adoration that I stopped short. My reflection in his eyes was distorted and ugly, a funhouse version of me. My heart stopped beating for a second.

This couldn't be Jus. He'd never, from first meeting onward, looked at me like that. With desire, with want, with admiration, with love, yes. But never with anything as twisted and ugly as disgust and betrayal.

Outwardly Jus was too calm. Silent fury was the scariest kind. Jus was calculating and analytical. His eyes narrowed. The gears turned, but to the wrong conclusion.

Rage and hurt rolled off him and filled the room with tension so oppressive I could barely breathe. He let go of the bunch of balloons. Opened his fingers and let them go, done with them. Done with me? They were weighted with a shiny blue plastic anchor and fell to the floor with a startling thud and a racket of rattling Mylar. And then blew in the breeze created by the air conditioning, rustling harbingers of relationship death.

"*Fuck*, Kay." Justin's voice was tight, constrained, violent in its calm stillness. More lethal and frightening than if he'd yelled and shouted. He clenched his fists. "I *loved* you."

Verb tense was everything, and he was using past tense. "Jus—"

His voice broke. "I loved you beyond *reason*. I'd hoped..." He slapped my cell phone on the console table and scooped up Data.

"Jus!" I grabbed his arm. "This isn't what it looks like."

"What does it look like, Kay? Like I'm the dumbest douchebag on the planet?" He shook me off, turned, and strode toward the door with Data cuddled in his arms.

Sensing something was wrong, Data barked unhappily and whined, appealing to me to do something, like a child caught in a bad divorce.

"Don't leave!" I reached for Jus and got caught in a tangle of balloon ribbons.

He brushed me aside and kept walking as I freed myself.

"You can't leave! Let me explain! You have to listen!" I turned over my shoulder to appeal to Lazer again.

He was staring at the balloons with a look of shock and some odd emotional combination on his face. Awe? Disgust? Praise?

A wave of nausea rolled over me. I swallowed a gag. *No. No. Not now!*

"Do something! *Tell* him, Lazer!" I said, fighting back the rising tide in my throat. If I sounded choked up, it was because I was. In so many ways, including literally.

Lazer shook his head, took a step toward me, and grabbed my arm. "Let him go, Kayla. Give him time to get his head out of his ass and think straight." He glared at Jus and puffed up, going alpha dog on me.

Jus didn't look back. The elevator arrived just as my stomach lurched again. I had Hobson's choice—run after the guy I loved and hurl all over him. Which might, or might not, stop him. Depending on how determined he was to leave. Or dash to the bathroom and hope I wasn't too late to hit the toilet. Either way, I was about to retch big time. Vomiting on Jus wasn't likely to make him any happier with me. Or see my point any more clearly. I opted for the bathroom, wrenched free from Lazer, and ran for it.

I puked until I was as empty inside as my heart. When the wave of morning sickness finally passed, I was shaky and paler than usual after an episode. I rinsed my mouth and wiped my face. And dashed out, hoping to still catch Jus even if I had to run out in the street in my underclothes. Hoping he was going slowly, wanting me to catch him. Hoping he'd turned around and come back and was waiting in the living room for me.

I had a momentary image of myself in the news. *Trouble in paradise? Billionaire Justin Green's crazed young wife runs desperately after him through the streets of Bellevue in her underwear. Story at six.*

Stupid notoriety! I took a deep, shaky breath.

When I came out of the bathroom, only Lazer was sitting in the living room. With a drink in his hand, swirling it so the ice clinked against the glass.

He watched me rush toward the door with calm curiosity. "You're too late. He's gone. He peeled out of the parking garage in a fury. I saw him blast down the road." He pointed in the general direction of the street below.

"Which way did he go?" I balanced on the balls of my bare feet, ready to chase after him.

Lazer raised a single eyebrow. "Does it matter? He can get to the freeway either direction. And from there, anywhere."

He studied me with a calm tenseness. Like he was worried I was going to burst into tears. "The way he was driving, the best thing you can do now is pray he doesn't kill himself. Or someone else. Or both. If you're lucky, he'll get pulled over. The cops will pull his license and drag his sorry butt home."

Lazer could be such an ass.

"You're so reassuring." My legs were about to give out. I grabbed my phone from the console table where Jus had left it and collapsed in a chair opposite Lazer.

"Don't even think about texting him! Until he's ready, he'll ignore it. Or delete it. He's not ready to hear what you have to say. And certainly in no mood to believe it."

He paused. "And if you think he's going to call, you *are* an optimist. Though I have to say, Jus doesn't usually overreact like this. He didn't walk in on anything *that* damning." Lazer frowned. "I've been caught in many situations that were much more compromising..."

I ignored Lazer as I looked at my phone and read the email from Britt that was on the screen.

Congrats, girl! Way to take advantage of the situation. You got pregnant ASAP!! Just like I told you to. Hook him for life. His money is yours. Did you flush the pills like I said? Ha ha! Whatever you do from now on doesn't matter. You're set for life! Money, money, money!!

"No. No. No no no, *no*!" I couldn't breathe. Having the air sucked out of me was becoming a habit I would gladly break if I could.

Why? Why would Britt email me something this damning? Something that in the wrong hands, and out of context, could be so totally misconstrued? She knew better.

Jus had been holding my phone when he'd walked in and thrown it on the table with enough rancor to try to break it. He must have read this message. He *had* to have read it!

Which explained so much. No wonder he'd taken the situation *completely* wrong. I'd hit him with a one-two sucker punch. He wouldn't know Britt was teasing. But why would she email me this message now? And he couldn't know that what was going on between Lazer and me was absolutely nothing. Piled on each other...

I felt about to throw up again. Not from morning sickness this time. I was heartsick. How was I going to fix this? How would he *ever* believe me?

"Kayla?" Lazer had set his drink down.

"Damn it!" I threw my phone across the room with the full intention of cracking its screen. But Jus, damn him, had bought me one of those covers that made it simply indestructible. He'd probably regretted the same thing. The phone bounced and came to a rest coyly face up, none the worse for the wear.

Lazer stared at me. "What does everyone have against that phone?" He got out of his chair.

I was out of mine and on his heels. But he retrieved it before I could stop him. He held the phone out of my reach and read that email while I tried to grab it out of his hands like I was in junior high and he was a boy who was teasing me.

His face went to stone. "Every billionaire's nightmare." He sounded sympathetic. But whether for Jus or me was up for debate. "We never know for sure if the woman we love loves us or our money. And Jus with no prenup, I'm assuming. Given the nature of your sudden marriage." He paused. Opened his mouth. Shut it.

Lazer at a loss for words. The world really was spinning backward.

"What will you do with your half of Justin's share of Flash?" he said at last, so calmly and deadpan I almost missed that he was teasing.

"She's *joking*!" I held my hand out for the phone. "Britt's joking. What can I say? She has a warped sense of humor. She's joked about it since the beginning. But I would never...I don't want Justin's money!"

He handed the phone back to me.

I clutched his arm. "*You* believe me, right? You have to believe me."

"That's becoming your catch phrase today."

I searched his eyes, hoping one damn person in this world believed me right now. And since it obviously wasn't Jus, praying that one person was Lazer Grayson. If he didn't, I was going to collapse. I needed his help convincing Jus that *nothing* was going on between us. If I lost Lazer's support, I was really and truly sunk.

"I wouldn't take his money," I said. "If Jus doesn't believe me, I'll walk away with nothing."

"Not smart, Kayla," Lazer said softly. "You have to think of the baby, too. Its father should support it. He has a legal *obligation* to provide for it. Which makes your grand gesture, however honestly felt, completely empty." He sounded halfway condemning.

I stared at him, resisting the urge to lash out at him. "There's no way I can win this, is there?"

"Assuming it's Justin's—"

"Of course it's Justin's! Do I even have to say it? Whose else would it be?" I shrieked, my voice pitching near that range that only dogs could hear.

"Well, you *did* throw yourself at me." His voice was serious, but his expression was teasing.

It was clear he was trying to be kind and break the tension, in his own perverse way. I was an emotional, hormonal wreck, so I didn't exactly appreciate his sense of humor right then. This wasn't funny.

"What am I going to do, Lazer? You have to help me get him back!" I covered my eyes with my hands and sobbed.

Lazer pulled me into his arms and held me. "You know, this is really the wrong thing to do. If he comes back and sees us like this—"

Justin

I squealed out of Bellevue, hell on wheels. At that precise moment, I was blinded by rage, fear, heartbreak. I hated Lazer. But what had I expected? I should have known Kayla would choose him over me. It had never been a fair fight. I just hadn't thought she'd betray me for money, too. Get pregnant to get more of mine. She wasn't satisfied with ten million and the chance to go after Lazer in less than a year?

Was she afraid of losing him in that time? Or just tired of pretending to love me?

I wondered if Kay had just shot her chances with Lazer all to hell. Would he want a woman who was pregnant with my kid? I couldn't picture Lazer as a dad, especially to a kid who wasn't his. I couldn't picture him with a pregnant woman at all.

Which raised the question—was the baby mine?

I laughed softly to myself without mirth. Kay wouldn't be dumb enough to try to pass a baby off as mine that wasn't. She'd have to know that if there were ever any question, I'd demand a paternity test. If she'd been planning to leave me for Lazer all along, she would have made sure the child was mine. Billions depended on it.

Which, in an odd way, should have comforted me. Odds were she hadn't slept with Lazer. At least not until she was sure she was pregnant with my baby. The thought of her and Lazer together made me sick. I trembled with rage.

Could Kay be such a fine actor? She'd sure as hell fooled me in Italy. But now everything she'd done was suspect. Had she staged her rugby accident to cut our honeymoon short and keep me from touching her more than necessary?

Every geek-guy insecurity I'd ever had rose to the surface. All this money. Shit! All this money, nothing more than a curse. I would never be certain of any woman's love. I thought I'd found genuine love with Kay. If she could betray me, how would I ever trust another woman?

And now this baby. This morning I'd been delirious with happiness. Now it tied me to a faithless woman. I had to think. I had to decide. I was too blinded by rage and hurt to think clearly right now.

Somehow I ended up back at Flash. I pulled the car into my reserved spot, turned off the engine, and pounded the steering wheel. I was stunned to be at Flash. I didn't remember the drive at all. And damned lucky I hadn't been pulled over. I had a vague memory of blasting through a red light at an intersection monitored by cameras. I could expect a ticket. Shit. Like I cared.

I was in deep trouble. Without Kay to vouch for the validity of our marriage, I was at the imposter's mercy. And if Kay wanted more money, she had the power to blackmail me for it now.

I took a deep breath, grasping for my coping mechanisms. When I was young, I'd been bullied to the point of breaking. As a bullying victim, there are two ways to fight back. Go completely crazy on your attackers. So crazy they're afraid of you. I was too physically small to apply that method with much success. And not violent enough by nature.

Or ruin your opponents after the fact of the attack in a way that lets them know, subtly, it was you. Though they can't prove it. And that you're capable of more, much more. They have to fear reprisal. You have to be smart. Wily. Devious. *Patient.* The guys who harassed me eventually learned that bad crap happened to them after messing with me. Too often to be coincidental.

My phone buzzed in my pocket. *A text.* My heart stopped. My hand shook as I pulled it out. I didn't know what I was hoping for. Yes, I did. Kay reaching out. A text was better than nothing at all.

I replayed the scene at the penthouse. The worst part. All right, not *the* worst part. *One* of the worst parts—she turned and ran away rather than chase after me. Yeah, I was upset and being a douche. But I wasn't worth going after? She gave up that easily on me? On us?

I looked at the phone.

From Dex. *Awesome news. I found her! She's still in Reno.*

I took a deep breath. All right then. Change of plans. If Kay didn't love me—I choked up at the thought—I had to disable the imposter *now.* No more waiting around. And then deal with Kay. I realized then that I'd been such a fool in love that I'd actually handed Kay more power than the ID thief had.

I was going to Reno to confront that bitch once and for all. Find out who and what were behind the girl I'd really married. Find out what she wanted. Like I didn't already know—what every other woman on the planet wanted, my money.

I texted Dex back. *Great. It's off to Reno.*

When?

First flight I can get. Get me the details. I'll look for them in the usual spot. Is everything in place? Are we ready to move?

As ready as we can be. I thought you wanted to wait until 90 days were up?

Something's come up. I need to act now.

Oh, shit, man, what?

It's personal.

There was a pause in our text conversation. I saw the thought bubbles while Dex typed, but he wasn't hitting send.

Trouble in paradise with my cousin?

Don't ask. I don't want to put you in the middle.

Since when have I cared about being caught in the crossfire? I want in. I'm going to Reno one way or another. I have my cousin to protect either way. Anyway, I've been in on this adventure too long to miss the grand finale. And I hate to say it—Kidding! No, I don't—you need me to run the scam on the scam artist. Who else can you trust? Who else has the skills? You don't want to let anyone else in on the secret now. Text me the details. I'll meet you at the airport.

I replied, *You have my birthday party to go to.*

So do you. You're a more important guest than I am. I'll text Lala my regrets. See you in a few.

I grabbed Data, jumped out of the car, and beeped it to lock it. Then I strode into Flash like I owned it. Oh, wait. I did.

Marla spotted me. "Hey, birthday boy! I thought you were out for the day?"

"I was." I forced myself to smile. "But you know Flash. She's a jealous mistress. She doesn't like sharing me with my personal life."

I was doing my damned best to put on a good face. But Marla picked up on something. She glanced at Data, who barked a greeting. "Is it take your dog to work day and I missed it?"

Yeah. Taking Data had been an impulse I was already regretting. I was too upset to leave her with Kay. What was I going to do with her now? "I have to take her to the groomer." Feeble lie.

Marla nodded and patted me on the shoulder. "It's your day. Take some time for yourself."

Yeah. Sure. It really was my day. From golden birthday to shredded paper birthday in a matter of minutes.

Ophie was at her desk. She looked up when I walked in, surprised. Then her face lit up with genuine delight. "Jus, what are you doing back?"

I hated myself for being so damned happy that *some* woman, any woman, was glad to see me. Ophie wore her adoration for me as plainly as one of her decorative scarves. She wasn't Kay. Never would be. But she was smart and loyal. And so into me it was almost painful.

I made a fist and walked past, calling over my shoulder. "I have a job for you. Come into my office."

She followed me in, too loyal to question me.

I shut the door behind her and set Data down to run around the office.

Ophie looked at me with limpid eyes. What the hell was so special and romantic about limpid eyes, anyway? It just meant clear. So? She had clear eyes? And yet they were. Clear and searching and sympathetic. Concerned for me. And in my current state, that meant something to me.

"I have to go to Reno." I looked down into those eyes and wondered for the first time since Kay'd come into my life what it would be like to kiss Ophie. What would it be like to be with a woman who worshiped me? With a woman I didn't have to win?

My ego was battered and bruised. I felt the balm of her gaze on me.

I cleared my throat and the thought. "Book me a chartered flight out. I'd like to leave as soon as possible. Within the hour. Two if absolutely necessary. I'll pay extra. Anything it takes. And book Data into the best dog-sitting kennel in the city." I hated to leave her in a kennel. But right now that was the lesser of two evils. I could have called Magda. But that seemed like too much of an imposition.

Ophie frowned gently, lines of concern on her face. She glanced at Data and back to me. "I haven't heard of any trouble."

I left her curiosity hanging.

Her forehead puckered. She laid a hand gently on my arm. "It's your birthday, Jus. Your wife is throwing you a big party tonight. Can't it wait?" She hesitated and bit her lip in the way Kay often did. "You don't want to disappoint her—"

"To hell with Kay!" The words burst out with more force than I intended. I took a deep breath and ran my hand through my hair, trying to get control of myself. "Business comes first."

Ophie nodded, her eyes sympathetic. "Will Riggins be going with you? Will he need arrangements?"

I shook my head. "Just me." I paused. What about Dex? "And maybe another. I'll need hotel accommodations, too. Book me in the usual suite."

"For how long?" she said, gazing up at me.

Her perfume wafted up to me, reminding me of Kay. I swallowed hard against the memories and the hurt that thoughts of Kay evoked.

"I don't know. A week? Start with that." I nodded, dismissing her to accomplish her task.

She nodded, too, and hesitated. "Do you need me to go with you? I'd be happy to." She paused, her hand still on my arm. "If you need me."

Did I need her? What the hell did I need? I'd thought I needed Kay.

Ophie knew how to be discreet.

"It's short notice. I'm not that kind of boss—"

She squeezed my arm. "I don't have any plans. I don't mind. Not at all."

I nodded. Or maybe I was.

CHAPTER TWO

Kayla
Even as Lazer tried to calm me down, my phone began buzzing with texts.

From Britt. *What is Justin doing back at work? I thought he left for the day?*

I couldn't even answer that one. Too angry and upset.

From my sorority sister Morgan. *Hugs, sweetie. Has Justin left you? It's all over social media! But they can be brutal, vicious liars. #Jus&KayDone #JusGreenAvailable? #AnotherCelebMarriageFail*

I took a look at my social media accounts and it was true. They were full of the news. It was even on the celebrity gossip blogs.

*Seattle flash sale fashion billionaire Justin Green
was caught on a traffic cam running a red light after
leaving his Bellevue penthouse in a hurry this afternoon. Neighbors who saw him in the parking garage
report that he was upset as he jumped into his sports
car and peeled out of the garage. A little birdie told us
his friend and mentor Lazer Grayson was seen going
up to the penthouse shortly before Justin arrived home
unexpectedly. Rumors have flown for months that
there may be more than friendship between Mr. Grayson and Mrs. Green. Has he finally come between Justin and Kayla for good?*

I showed it to Lazer. He shook his head. "Bastards."

I was furious and trembling with anger that was
quickly turning to rage. "Who told on us? Obviously
this snooty building doesn't have the high privacy
standard that Carl enforces at my apartment." When I
looked like I was going to throw the phone again, Lazer
pried it out of my hand.

"I think this has suffered enough trauma for one
day."

"What do I do about Justin's birthday party?" I said
to Lazer. "The caterers will be here in another hour. If
I hurry I can cancel—"

Lazer set the phone down and grabbed me by both
hands. "Absolutely not. If you cancel this party, you
verify the rumors. You give them exactly what they
want, an admission of guilt."

"How can I throw a birthday party without the
guest of honor? What if Jus doesn't show up?" I was
petrified that he wouldn't. And worried he would. The

last thing we needed was a scene in front of our family and friends.

"What if he doesn't?" Lazer shrugged.

"You haven't seen the birthday cakes. They're geared toward announcing our new little bundle of joy." I blinked back tears. "How can I announce something like that by myself?"

"You can always run to the grocery store and pick up a new cake quick," he said with dark humor.

I shot him a black look. I wasn't in the mood for funny. There was no way I could entertain at the billionaire's level with grocery-store-bought cake.

Lazer held up his hands in self-defense. "If he doesn't show, you tell the guests yourself. Show them how committed you two are to being a family and staying together.

"We'll make up a story about Justin suddenly being called away on urgent business. The key is for us to go on like business as usual. Anyone who's known Justin since he started Flash won't be surprised he'd put the company before his own birthday interests. They'll applaud you for being such a supportive wife." He looked deep into my eyes. "Do you want Justin back?"

I nodded, heart breaking. "That goes without saying, doesn't it?"

He had the good grace not to comment.

I took a deep breath. "Damn it, Lazer! Of all the times we could have been caught when there actually was a reason for Jus to be jealous and now he walks in on us when everything was totally innocent. It isn't fair!"

Lazer squeezed my hands. "Since when did life promise to be fair?"

I had no answer. But that was his point, wasn't it?

"Look, if you want Justin back, you're going to have to fight for him. Be prepared to put on the show of your life tonight. You'll have to be glittering and vivacious. Happy. Excited about this pregnancy. Effusive. Gushing about Justin and having his baby! And how wonderful everything is!" He was putting girly inflection on everything on purpose. It was annoying in its false perkiness and near mockery. "Everything the happily married expectant mom should be.

"No one can suspect the truth. No one should even *guess* there's any hint of trouble between you. Or that I'm part of it.

"When I show up, acting my part of Justin's friend and mentor, tongues will wag. At first. After that, everyone will go home laughing about tabloid news. Leaving everyone wondering how the rumors could possibly be true." He gave my hands a shake and another squeeze. "How good's your acting?"

Acting. Again. I sighed. "Pretty damn convincing when it needs to be." Wasn't that the truth? "Lazer?"

"Yes?"

"Bring a date tonight," I said, wiping my eyes. "As hot a date as you can find."

"You want me to find a date at this late notice?" He laughed like it was a challenge he looked forward to.

"Is that a problem?"

He shrugged.

"Pay one if you have to," I said.

"It won't come to that." He grinned, full of a kind of egotistical charm.

If Jus really wouldn't come back to me...

No. Lazer and I weren't meant to be. I wouldn't give up so easily. I wanted Jus. I *would* get him back.

"Make sure she and you are convincing." I tried not to sniffle. "We have to squelch these rumors."

"Let me handle it." Lazer turned me toward the bedroom. "Now, go wipe your eyes and put on the outfit you were planning to wear. Reapply your makeup. And smile."

I paused to look at him. "What are you going to do?"

"Sneak out of here without getting caught."

Justin

Staring at Ophie, I made a split-second decision. Getting back at Kay by getting with Ophie was reckless. As angry and hurt as I was, common sense stopped me. Yeah, I could have used an ego boost. But I'd already screwed up too many times. I couldn't take the chance that Ophie would find out what I was really up to in Reno. I needed the freedom to bring down the imposter. And then...

The hell if I knew. For now I had to focus my anger and energy on one thing.

"I need you here," I said.

Her face fell. She recovered quickly and nodded. "Then why do you need a dog sitter? I'll watch Data."

I shook my head. "Thanks, but no. I don't want to put you out."

"You're not putting me out. I love animals!"

I shook my head. "Call the sitter."

Ophie nodded reluctantly. "I'll take her over myself later. Right now, let me get you that plane."

Ophie's organizational skills never failed to amaze me. Ophie had a plane, and a dog sitter, lined up within the hour, just as I'd requested. Dex met me at the airport. By unspoken agreement, guided by prudence and a sense of playing spy, neither of us could talk about the mission while we were in public, on the plane, or anywhere else anyone could overhear. In that regard, hanging with Dex was like pretending to be married to Kay.

Every time I thought about her, the hurt welled up along with rage.

Dex slapped me on the back. "We'll talk later, man."

I gave him a dark, skeptical look. "I don't feel like talking."

"No? But plans must be made." Dex winked.

"What excuse did you make to Kay?" Morbid curiosity was hell.

Dex shrugged. "The truth—I'd been called out of town." He laughed wickedly.

Kayla

Dex called out of town? With Justin? At least my cousin was kind enough to let me know and not leave me hanging as to whether Jus would attend his own party. So now it was clear—Jus had abandoned me. Flown the city and the coop of domesticity. Left me to deal with the wolves of society alone. To tame the suspicions and gossipmongers.

He didn't deserve for me to save his ass, but I was determined to do it anyway. Out of a perverse sense of pride. I wasn't going to be dumped by Justin Green.

I was in no emotional shape to throw a party. Broken hearts didn't put me in the best partying mood. Added to that was my fury, whether completely warranted or not, with my best friend. How could she be so stupid?

My morning sickness had taken a turn for the worse. I was literally sick and tired. And figuratively sick and tired of pretending about everything. Of living in a world where nothing was real. Everything was faked. And the good deeds and points I made counted for nothing.

I made up my mind—Lazer was right. I was going to share the news of my pregnancy at Justin's party whether he showed up or not. And since he was supposedly on a plane out of town, "not" was the most likely scenario. Though he had enough money to turn the plane around if he wanted. Anyway, one less secret to keep. And sympathies would run on my side on this one. How dare he abandon his pregnant wife when she'd planned such a perfect party for him? What a douche!

Every breakup has it stages of grief. There's shock, heartbreak, and denial. Which are almost always followed by anger. Righteous anger was coming on strong for me. I fed off it. Its energy would get me through the party. I just hoped it didn't turn my baby into a monster. Or give me a major case of heartburn. Ha! So aptly named in this case.

Okay, so from Justin's perspective, things *had* looked bad when he'd walked in on me. Did that mean it was okay for Jus to jump to conclusions? To assume the worst? To think that I would lie to him about loving him? Get pregnant on purpose for his money? Did he not know me at all? Wasn't he the one who'd had to convince me to take his money and this wife gig in the first place? Was his memory so short? Was he so insecure that he couldn't believe I loved him?

He was being a douche! A complete and utter idiot. If he was going to be that way, I would...I would...I wanted to slap him. Shove him. Scream at him. Throw a tantrum. So, yes, my inner five-year-old was raging.

I resisted the urge to text him and tell him where he could go and what he could do. In other words, commit relationship suicide. Lazer's warning stopped me. If I texted, I was going to say something I would regret later. Maybe forever. Right now, I had a job to do— stop the spread of gossip. Put a good face on things until the father of my child came to his senses. *If* he came to his senses.

No, *when*. When, when, when. It *had* to be when.

All right, I was being a flipper and a flopper. But that's the way heartbreak was, wasn't it? You're sometimes fatalistic and sometimes overly optimistic. Emotional turmoil is nonsensical by nature.

In my raging state, I began to wonder if I could live with a guy who had so little faith in me and my love for him. I didn't have time to be philosophical. I had to get moving!

I followed Lazer's instructions and got dressed. In my sexiest happy-birthday-baby dress. Ha! Double entendre there. Jus would be sorry he'd missed seeing me in this. It was one of my Italian purchases that would soon be on the Flash site. And relegated to my closet as I developed a baby bump. But that was me—always promoting Flash like a good little spouse.

I reapplied my makeup with care. Vamping it up. If the dogs of gossip were going to howl, they might as well have something to howl about. I put on a bright face and a dazzling assortment of Italian gold jewelry. Highly appropriate for Justin's golden birthday celebration. I even rehearsed what I was going to say to Britt. Which only fueled the fires of anger and indignation.

Then I dragged that rattling monstrosity of Mylar baby congrats balloons out to the balcony where they wouldn't be the first things the guests saw and spoil my big announcement and sympathy play.

On the balcony, they blew in the gentle breeze, bumping against each other like playful siblings hellbent on aggravating their parents with all the grating noise they made. The balloons mocked me with their cheerful message and extravagance. In a fit of anger, I stomped inside to the kitchen, grabbed a pair of kitchen shears, tromped outside, bent, and cut the balloons loose from their base.

I held them for a second, clutched in my fist so tightly my knuckles turned white. Rage was a powerful thing. At that moment I hated Jus. I hated him because it was better than falling apart. I couldn't afford to cave to my emotions and break down now. Too much depended on it. I stood and slowly opened my fingers. *Oops!* The balloons slipped out of my grasp. How sad.

I watched them float over the balcony railing and into the sky above Bellevue, feeling they were somehow symbolic of my situation. They glinted in the evening sun, drifting upward and away in a much more gentle manner than Justin's love had left me. Suddenly, they caught a thermal and took off, rising higher and higher. Out of my reach. Wasn't that the way with everything in my life right now?

I had a moment's panic as I imagined the media getting hold of this gesture of mine. Fortunately, squeezed out by rage, the panic fled quickly enough.

As I turned to go into the penthouse, I tripped on the anchor. I grabbed it, tempted to hurl it over the balcony, too. Only the thought of hurting some innocent bystander on the street below stopped me. Rage makes you blind. It had blinded me earlier. I hadn't seen the gold pendant necklace looped around the blue anchor. A big heart with a little heart cuddled inside.

Ah. Mommy and baby. With no daddy heart, I might add.

Fine, Jus! Leave me with this sentimental gesture to break my heart again. I swallowed the lump in my throat. And put on my defiant face as I unhooked the necklace and put it on. *I'll wear your token of love and show everyone.*

I may need to pawn this later, I thought. I was that mad and upset.

My perpetually early, eager parents showed up first, carrying a huge gift box and worrying over it. And me. It was clear from the moment they arrived that they were uncomfortable. And concerned for me. Dad was eyeing me with that physician's look, the one where he assessed my color and tried to determine my overall health. I wondered if he could see the nausea looming just below the surface.

"What do you get a billionaire?" Mom whispered to me with a nervous titter in her voice. "It's impossible!"

My answering smile felt brittle. It was so hard to be pleasant when you were angry. "It will be *fine*, Mom. Jus is easy to please. He'll be happy you thought of him. It's all in the thought."

And right now, he was full of bad thoughts. But I kept that to myself.

Mom looked around the penthouse like she was looking for evidence of a theft. "Where *is* our wonderful son-in-law?" She sounded a little too suspicious.

She'd heard the gossip. She had to have.

Wonderful, indeed! He's just abandoned your daughter! I wanted to scream. *And your grandbaby.* Was it possible to be too snarky and cynical in your thought life? At that moment there wasn't enough snark in the world for me to command.

My smile started to slip. It was taking conscious thought to keep it in place. What I wanted and what I had to do were two very different things. I *wanted* to crawl into my mother's arms, tell her how horribly Jus had treated me. And listen to her comforting *there-theres* while she patted my back and I cried my eyes out over that bastard Jus. I wanted to hear her complete sympathy. I wanted her motherly indignation on my behalf. I wanted her to treat me like she had after all my high school breakups.

Crying over Jus! It was almost unfathomable. The college me would have laughed in my face at the thought.

But of course, I was locked in this fake happy marriage. It was nothing more than a job, after all, though, right? And I needed a high score on my job performance review to get that ten-million-dollar payout. Especially now. Damn Jus! I was so mad at him.

I managed to hold my smile in place and look as absolutely placid as if I was sailing through a happy day. "The birthday guy was called out of town this afternoon."

My mom's eyes narrowed with suspicion. Motherly instinct sucked sometimes with its pinpoint accuracy. "But...how can you have a birthday party without the birthday person?"

I shrugged. "Billionaires! They're so eccentric." I winked at Mom. "Seriously. Jus was devastated he couldn't be here. But he wanted the party to go on. At this point, we were going to be paying for everything anyway. Our guests may as well enjoy it!"

So much fake enthusiasm. So little heart behind it.

My mom grabbed my arm and pulled me close to whisper in my ear. "Is everything *okay* between you and Justin? The news is full of your...unhappiness."

She must have been upset. She couldn't even bring herself to name the gossip.

I stiffened. I didn't want to disappoint her. At the same time, at that moment, I almost wanted to come completely clean. And save my pride. *How could he break my heart, Mom? He never had it. This is just a business relationship.*

"Dad and I are on your side, no matter what. You know that," she whispered to me. "You rushed into marriage...maybe a little too quickly. To a young man you hadn't seen in years. If he isn't the guy you thought he was...well, you're our daughter. We're behind you."

There was that stupid lump in my throat again. I had to swallow it before it got the best of me and gave me away. There were no true confessions on the agenda. Tonight I had to hold my tongue, keep my head high, and fool everyone. Most especially our parents.

"Thanks, Mom!" Which I genuinely meant. "But you can't believe everything you hear on the news. Especially on those gossip segments. I've heard the latest. I've learned to ignore it. They make up such outrageous stuff! Next they'll have me having an alien's baby!"

Wasn't I? Jus was certainly alien to me right now. And we were alienated.

I laughed to make my point. "Jus and I are *fine. Perfectly* happy together."

Justin

As soon as we were airborne, I poured myself a drink. With the full intention of getting bombed. How do you take the edge off a broken heart?

Dex watched me, his eyes bright and searching. He grabbed my arm. "In the conference room. Let's go."

I grabbed my glass and the bottle as he pulled me into the private room and shut the door.

"All right. So talk. What happened between you and Lala?" He crossed his arms and studied me with an intense, piercing expression.

I fell into a leather desk chair next to the conference table, downed my drink, and poured myself another while I waited for a buzz to kick in. "She cheated on me. With Lazer Grayson."

Dex cocked an eyebrow. "Lala cheated?"

I nodded, miserable with an ache so deep even the booze didn't numb it. I swallowed the lump in my throat.

"That doesn't sound like her. She's a one-man girl. A serial monogamist. The Lala I know would have dumped you first before moving on."

"I'm her husband," I said, irritated that he was taking her side. Though what did I expect? They were family. Taking Dex along might have been a mistake. "Short of divorce, how was she going to dump me?"

"Oh, I don't know, dickhead," Dex said with absolutely no sympathy at all. "Your 'marriage' is just a business arrangement. All she had to do was say she's done having sex with you, let's keep it platonic, and move on."

Dex had never pulled his punches.

"She got pregnant," I said. "Just so she could get a bigger piece of my assets."

Dex shook his head. "Dude! I don't see what you're so upset about. Didn't I tell *you* to knock *her* up if you want to keep her?" he argued in his typically logical fashion.

"This just saves you the trouble of subterfuge. If this is true, you have leverage, man. She won't want to let go of that baby. She'll agree to almost anything to keep you from trying to take it away. This is epically good news." He patted me on the back. "Congrats, Papa! And happy birthday to you. This is the best gift she could have given you."

I stared at him.

"Out of curiosity, how do you *know* she planned it? Lala had several pregnancy scares in college. None of those were planned."

I frowned, confused. Dex, with his inexplicable logic, was actually making me feel somewhat better. I spilled the whole story while he listened in silence, without interrupting.

When I was finished, he shook his head. "No. I don't buy it. For one thing, Lala's friends may not be geniuses like us. But they aren't stupid, either. Especially Britt.

"Little Miss Emotional Intelligence? Sending a dumbass email like that? That's an amateur mistake she'd never make."

He paused. "Would I put it past her to give Lala the advice to get preggo with your baby? Absolutely not. It's damn good advice, if I do say so myself.

"Cheer up, buddy! You and Lala have more in common than you thought." He looked genuinely pleased at the thought, and proud of his cousin. "You've been working toward the same goal. But to write the plan out and email it to Lala, taking a chance you'd see it and foil the plan? No way. Not Britt." He shook his head.

"I know what I saw. It was right there on her phone. I can hack into her email and show you. She uses the world's simplest passwords." I grabbed my phone. Within seconds I was into her account. I showed it to Dex and watched him read it.

He shrugged. "Still not buying it. There has to be another explanation. Something that makes sense."

I brushed his comment aside. "Not everything makes sense. And her cheating? I caught her in the act."

"You caught her being hugged." His voice was stern.

He grabbed the bottle away from me while I tried to pour another drink. The liquor spilled in a stream over the desk and filled the room with a boozy smell. I reached for a napkin to wipe it up.

He caught my hand. "Listen to me. Your 'marriage' was nothing more than an arrangement. Lala never had to sleep with you. There was nothing forcing her to be exclusive with you. If she'd wanted to be with Lazer, she would have told you and gone back to the original agreement."

I wrenched my hand free and took the bottle back. "She doesn't love me." My voice cracked like I was still in junior high. Or maybe that was college for me.

"I forced her hand." I tried, but couldn't swallow my guilt. "I forced her into this marriage." I was on the edge. "Shit, Dex. I forced her."

Dex squatted next to me. "What did you do?"

CHAPTER THREE

Kayla

And so the party was going swimmingly. Sickeningly
well, actually. The caterer was a hit. The waiters efficient. The band I'd hired so we could have a live rendition of "Happy Birthday" and Jus could show off and
sing with them held to just the right volume to make
conversation comfortable.

After a tense moment when they were introduced
and eyed each other like competitors in *Family Feud*,
Justin's parents and mine were conversing pleasantly.
Watching them, I didn't have any illusions they'd ever
be close friends. The way things were going, it didn't
matter in the long run. Or even the near short term,
for that matter. As long as they made it through the
evening.

Britt was late, fortunately. By the time she arrived I was so busy playing hostess I didn't have time for her. Which was great, because if I was around her too much I was bound to go off on her. And that would not be a good party scene.

Everyone asked where Jus was. I had to fake it and make excuses. Fortunately my acting skills had been honed by real-life method acting around the clock for these past months. I played dutiful wife with a passion and sweetness that was sickening even to me.

Lazer arrived with a former Miss Washington on his arm. A flashy auburn beauty in a dress that showed off just why she'd taken the title and won the swimsuit part of the competition. I found that I was surprisingly not jealous of her at all. Only in the fact that they were coupled up. And I was shockingly solo at my husband's party.

"I see you picked up a date," I whispered to Lazer when I got a chance.

"Short notice is never a problem for me," he said with a wicked, teasing glint in his eye. "How are you doing?"

"Acting the part," I said. "You two make a cute couple."

My stomach was unsettled. Morning sickness threatened to erupt, egged on by nerves. When it seemed like everyone had had enough hors d'oeuvres and was ready for cake, I had the caterers roll the cakes in on a serving cart.

Justin's birthday cake was a three-layer cake staggered on three separate tiered risers. It was decorated in gold fondant with a fourteen-karat gold number twenty-two on top and twenty-two long, tapered golden candles ready to be lit. It was so over the top, he would have loved it. I was mad at him for missing it. And this lovely, golden party I was throwing him. Cynically, I thought maybe I should snap a shot of it for him. So he could see what he was missing.

I had my waiters bring around trays of champagne in glasses with gold rims. Each glass had a small gold coin sitting at the bottom beneath the champagne bubbles. Yes, excess. That's what being a billionaire was about, wasn't it?

I had to do everything golden and extreme during this year. Maybe I didn't even have a year. At this rate, Jus and I would be lucky to make it to our regularly scheduled divorce. We sure weren't going to make it to our golden wedding anniversary. And my golden birthday had been when I was too young to remember it.

I stood next to the cake trolley and called the crowd to order by ringing a golden bell. When the crowd quieted down, I began my prepared speech.

"As Justin's new wife, I'm totally crazy about him. All of you here know that!" I grinned devilishly. "And maybe I'm just plain crazy." That much was true. "I wanted Justin's first married birthday to be his best birthday yet." I cleared my throat. A lump was threatening.

A few guests nodded their agreement.

"Well, I did my best, and have done my best, but work called Jus away at the last minute." I put on what I hoped was a pretty pout. Though it felt more like a scowl. "Everyone dreams of wealth and success, but to get it takes a lot of work. As Jus will agree."

People laughed politely.

"A lot of you here tonight brought Jus gifts, even though I specifically said not to." I frowned and pointed a few fingers around the room, teasingly chastising them. "Guilty. Guilty. Guilty."

More laughter.

"It's not that Jus doesn't deserve them." I had to force myself not to break up. And not to lash out, either. I balanced on a precarious emotional ledge. But if things were going to appear normal and happy between Jus and me, I had to deliver the speech I'd been planning to make before things blew up.

"We're all friends and family here. We all love Jus. It's just—what do you give a billionaire?

"Because this is our first birthday together, and it's Justin's golden birthday—twenty-two on the twenty-second—I wanted to give him something that no one else has. Something unique. One of a kind."

I grabbed a lighter the caterers had put next to his cake and began lighting his twenty-two candles. "But before I reveal my gift to him." I nodded to Riggins. "Let's sing Jus 'Happy Birthday.' I can't carry a tune. So Riggins is going to do the honors and lead us." I motioned to the band. "Is someone recording this?"

I got a thumbs-up.

"Good!" I looked around the room. "Will someone film this for Jus, too? We can all text him birthday wishes from our unique perspective so he'll feel like he was really here! He'd *love* that!"

Take that, Jus.

The band struck up "Happy Birthday." Riggins sang the lead. The rest of us sang in whatever key suited us. And somehow we made it through. Most people were enjoying themselves. Some of the oddness of having a birthday party for a guy who wasn't there was wearing off. When the song ended, people erupted in applause.

I rang the golden bell again and grabbed the golden lid of the cake plate on the small cake next to Justin's, ready for my reveal. "Bear with me. I'm not as narcissistic as this looks. Before we have cake, I have to share with you all what I got him. And, yes, Jus already knows and is thrilled." I laughed. "And maybe a little overwhelmed."

I pulled the lid off to reveal a baby-themed cake decorated with tiny feet in pink and blue. "I'm giving Jus the gift of fatherhood!

"To Jus! Happy birthday, baby! Don't work too hard! Wish you were here!" I raised my glass and took a sip.

I was rushed by our moms, who were suddenly in competition for hugs with questions flying. As the caterers cut the cake, I was swallowed by the well-wishing crowd. The moment would have been perfect. If Jus had been there.

Suddenly, I felt hot and nauseated. Suffocated. I broke free from the group and dashed for the bathroom. "Sorry, everyone!"

The women smiled knowingly. I heard someone say something about "must be a healthy pregnancy if she's sick already."

I made it just in time. This pregnancy was going to kill me. But the moms were excited. There was that, at least. And already making over me. Diana would personally whip her boy if he dumped the mother of her first grandchild. So the building-loyalty play was working.

When I came out of the bathroom, Britt was lying in wait. She pounced, grabbing my arm before I could escape. "You've been avoiding me! What's going on? And don't blame it on pregnancy hormones. I know that game."

I glared at her. "You!" I pointed my finger at her and tried not to sputter in my anger. "How could you be so stupid?"

"Stupid how?" She was glaring back. Britt wasn't some mellow puppy to be pushed around.

I grabbed her arm, pulled her into my bedroom, and closed the door so we could talk in private.

"What's really going on with you and Jus?" she said. "Why isn't he here? He came back to work this afternoon, called Ophie into his office, and flew out of there after ten minutes. He looked pissed. And hurt. Like someone had whipped him or stomped on his aorta or something. And since you're the only one with that power over him..."

That was the thing about Britt—her emotional IQ never failed her. And she was observant. So there was no use trying to fool her on this one.

"We're on the point of breakup. Because of you!" I pointed at her again and grabbed my phone from the nightstand where I'd left it. "And your damning email."

"What are you talking about?" she said. "*What* email?"

I brought it up and turned the phone around so she could read it.

"'Hook him for life. His money is yours. Did you flush the pills like I said? Ha ha! Whatever you do from now on doesn't matter. You're set for life! Money, money, money!'" she read aloud. "Who wrote this crap? It sounds like a melodrama."

"You did!" I pointed to the email header, thinking my life was a melodrama right at the moment. "It's from *your* email account."

"If I wrote that, it would be much better. More elegant." Understanding dawned on her. "He saw it?"

I nodded, too upset to speak.

She whistled softly. "So not good. But at least we're getting to the meat of the issue." She took the phone and shook her head. "It's from my account, but I didn't send it." She handed the phone back to me.

I made thin, angry eyes at her and bit back the tart, yet somehow salty, words on the tip of my tongue. I shook the phone at her. "Come on! No lies. Just admit to your screwup so we can make up and you can help me through this! This is like that time in junior high when you texted Corey and told him I was in love with him and then you denied doing it."

She took a deep, huffy type of breath and sighed heavily. "This is *nothing* like that. That was true. And I was just trying to help. This email is vindictive."

I shook the phone at her. "This message, this was the advice you gave me when we were first married!"

"Yeah! Exactly. So why would I text it to you now, out of the blue? That's ridiculous. Almost a total non sequitur. There's no conversational flow to it." She shook her head. "I've been working with you on Justin's birthday surprise for weeks. I've known you were pregnant all that time. So why would I just *now* text you this bullshit?"

I had no good answer, really. Because, actually, she made a good, logical point.

She grabbed the phone from my hand, disarming me before I tossed it across the room again. Or at her.

"Plus I'm not dumb enough to email something as damning and damaging to you when Justin could get hold of your phone and read it. Or hack into your email account and see it. The guy's a computer genius. I wouldn't trust anything as damning as this to any digital space in the world." She looked at the email again while I tried to grab the phone back.

She held it out of my reach. "Hold on! Hold on a minute. Not only does this not sound like me, it's from my work email account." She held the phone out for me to take. "See for yourself."

"What?" Blinded by rage again. She was right.

"You know me well enough. I never send personal crap from my work email. *Never.* It's a recipe for getting fired. Especially if you're talking about the boss."

I took a deep breath. The more she talked, the more out of character this whole event seemed for her.

"Hmmm." She put a hand to her chin, thinking. "I didn't turn my work computer on until after lunch. Remember? I was meeting with you for part of the

morning. And then I wasn't even at my desk all afternoon. I was in meetings." She looked at me significant-
ly, like Sherlock Holmes putting the pieces of a
mystery together, trying to identify the culprit.

"Anyone could have stopped by my desk and sent
this email," Britt said. "My computer isn't password
protected once I log in."

I was feeling sick again. "But who knows—"

"Ophie!" we said at the same time.

"Oh, crap!" I said. "The sneaky, eavesdropping
bitch! She *did* hear us that day at lunch. We have to get
this email off the server."

Britt's eyes narrowed. She looked relieved that I finally believed her. And about ready to kill Ophie for
attempting to murder our friendship and sabotage her
career. "That dastardly marriage saboteur!"

I went cold. "Jus brought my phone home to me today. At first I thought I must have accidentally left it at
your desk this morning when I stopped by. But now I
wonder..."

"She probably pinched it! And sent that email when
she knew Justin was on his way home to you, hoping
he'd take it the wrong way." Britt clenched her hands.
"He walked right into her trap. That's positively diabolical."

"And right in on me when I was in an apparently
compromising hug with Lazer." I explained the situation Jus had seen to Britt.

"So he walked out on you," she said when I was finished. "Small wonder." She nodded. "And came back to
the office upset. And you don't know where he is?"

"No, I know. He's with Dex on his way to Reno." I almost blew it then and told her the rest of the story about them going after the ID thief. I stopped just in time.

"Why Reno?" She looked puzzled.

"It's a good cover story for a drinking binge. You know, Flash has a distribution center there. They can gamble and carouse and get drunk while saving face by claiming they're on business."

Britt pursed her lips. "Okay, then. Let the boys play for a while. We have to stop Ophie from doing more damage." She paused. "And by the way—I think she has your dog. I saw her walking out of the office with her."

CHAPTER FOUR

Justin

The texts started coming in even before we landed, a digital aerial assault. Well coordinated. Birthday wishes. Pictures from my party. Riggins leading the crowd in an awful, off-key rendition of "Happy Birthday." Riggins did a great job. It was everyone else that was the problem.

Pictures of my over-the-top gold cake. How it could have been so ostentatious and yet so perfect and classy was beyond me. Kay had the knack. Video clips. Lazer with some auburn-haired beauty on his arm, the decoy date.

If they thought I was going to believe that act...

Kay announcing her pregnancy. My heart stopped beating for a second as I watched her speech. She was so damned hot. She faked her love for me so convincingly. And she was more conniving than I'd given her credit for. Everyone who mattered now knew about the baby. My mom got tears in her eyes.

I balled my fist. Touché, Kay! Well played. She was ingratiating herself with everyone. If this kept up, I would be the bad guy. The douche who tossed his pregnant wife aside.

I took a deep breath. Confessing to Dex had felt good. But now the effects of his pep talk had worn off. He didn't understand. I didn't just *want* Kay. I wanted her to love me. And she didn't. Despite my best efforts, she didn't.

I'd made a mistake in trusting her. The love of money is the root of all evil. Her love of me would have been our salvation.

I renewed my goal—get that imposter and make it impossible for her to damage either my reputation, or Flash's success. The second-quarter numbers would be announced soon. Bad press about my personal life would affect the stock valuation. I wasn't going to let this spook our investors or the market.

I shut my phone off. *Nice try, Kay.*

Kayla

The incident with Britt, and how easy it was for someone to frame her, and for me to get the wrong idea, taught me several lessons. One, never jump to conclusions. And two, give people who've proven themselves as loyal friends the benefit of the doubt. I was as guilty as Jus in assuming the worst of someone I loved who had been loyal to me. So, mistakes happen. Now I had to get my husband back. But first I had to get my puppy out of the clutches of the enemy.

Justin's birthday was Friday night. On Saturday morning, I dressed for battle and drove to Ophie's condo in downtown Seattle. With Britt riding shotgun for moral support. I'll say this for Jus, Ophie lived in the heart of the city in a high-rise condo with a view, which meant he paid her well.

The night before, Britt had related the entire scene she'd seen—Jus coming into the office carrying Data. Going into his. Calling Ophie in. Then coming out and handing Data over to Ophie. Her promise to take her to a dog sitter.

"What makes you think she didn't?" I'd asked Britt.

"The look on her face," Britt said. "She had no intention of parting with that dog." She'd paused. "I think using Data and winning her affection is the next step in her plan to get Justin for herself. She looked pretty smug, too. I was suspicious at the time, but I had nothing to back it up."

Britt's emotional IQ hadn't failed yet. On Saturday morning, I caught a break. I woke up to a call from Magda, wanting to know why Ophie needed to know the number of the breeder Jus had bought Data from and what kind of dog food we fed her.

Why, indeed? Britt had been right! Ophie had my puppy. I'd spent a long, lonely night with neither her nor Jus in my bed. Jus was out of reach right now, but I could get my dog back.

I pulled into Ophie's parking garage and had the valet park my car. They recognized it as one of Justin's and I immediately got the respect of someone who looked capable of leaving a big tip. Or complaining loudly like a bitch.

"What do we do now?" I said to Britt. "Doesn't she have to buzz us up?"

Britt rolled her eyes and looked at me like I'd gone soft since living the good life. "Have you lost all common sense? We draft in behind the first person we can, pretending we've forgotten our keys." She looked around. "This place is pretty busy. It shouldn't take long."

"Oh, right." Well, duh. We'd done this countless times before for various reasons. If you have to, you bat your eyes at some guy to let you in. Britt and I didn't look like crazy psychos or cat burglars, so we usually didn't have much trouble.

Sure enough, we'd waited less than five minutes before we trailed in behind some older guy who liked the way we looked and wasn't immune to our smiles. We took the elevator to Ophie's condo and got out in the hall. Britt stayed by the elevator, ready to man it for our escape. Yes, this was a first class caper we were pulling off. Look out, *Ocean's Eleven* We were that sneaky and prepared. Not.

Britt gave me a hug and I was off to Ophie's condo. The second I knocked on the door, barking erupted inside. Data's bark, to be exact. I'd become a doggy mom who recognized her child's voice. Data had a bark for everything. This one was her *Someone's at the door* bark. And I may have been a nervous doggy mommy imagining it, but I thought she sounded scared and confused and had a bit of "rescue me" in her yip.

Inside, Ophie yelled at her to be quiet. Ophie swung the door open. Her face was fierce and curious. Until she saw me and her expression turned to *Oh crap*. She slammed the door. But not quick enough. I stuck my foot in the door and brought it to a screeching halt. Fortunately, I'd been prepared enough to wear substantial shoes built for running. I pushed the door open again.

Ophie glared at me. "What are you doing here?"

Data came bounding toward me.

"Hey, baby!" I kneeled and scooped her up before Ophie could stop me. I cuddled her in my arms and cooed to her. "Did you have a bad night? Poor puppy! Mama's come to take you home." I kissed her doggy head and stroked her beneath her chin the way she liked.

I stood and glared back at Ophie. "In case it isn't obvious, I came to get my dog."

Ophie reached for her. "You can't do that! Jus entrusted her to me when he left you." Her tone was superior and cutting. Triumphant and evil at the same time. It was clear she meant to drive a knife into my heart.

Fortunately, I was girded with anger. "This is a community property state. Which makes Data as much mine as Justin's." I narrowed my eyes, trying to look menacing. "And I have it on good authority that Jus asked you to take her to a kennel."

"He was too upset to know what he wanted." She got up in my face. "After *you* betrayed him with Lazer." There was that victorious look again. "Yeah, Jus told me all about it."

I went cold to the pit of my stomach. My suspicions came together, making clarity out of the fog of suspicious circumstances. All those "accidental" meetings.

I stared at her, speechless for the moment, unable to believe how truly diabolical she'd been. Willing her to ramble on like the villain she was and spill all.

Instead, she glared back at me silently.

I got right back in her face, cradling Data against me to protect her puppy ears from the vile accusations that were about to spew. "You threw Lazer and me together." For once my voice was deadly calm.

She grinned. "Did I?" She laughed. "You give me too much credit. But if I had, I would have been doing you a favor. Your popular society bitch kind belongs with Lazer and his philandering ways. You and he are the perfect match. A beautiful storybook couple." Her eyes were hard.

"But Jus belongs with me." She tapped her chest. "We understand each other. We're the same social class. He only *thought* he wanted you. Because guys do when they're thinking with their dicks. But once the thrill wears off, guys like Jus realize they need a woman with brains and substance."

"*You*"—I pointed an accusatory finger at her—"sent him that email about the baby from Britt's computer." I held her gaze, watching for any signs she was lying.

"Prove it."

The bile was rising in my throat. Anger and hatred upset my stomach. "You're nothing but a sneaky eavesdropper. You overheard us in the restaurant."

"So you admit it's true!" She had that "I gotcha" look on her face.

"That was a joke." I swallowed hard as a round of morning sickness threatened. "It doesn't matter, though, what you think. Jus is mine now. I'm having his baby."

And then a wave of nausea rolled over me. My stomach lurched. Just like that I upchucked my bacon and eggs all over Ophie.

While she was too stunned to speak, I turned and ran with Data barking happily in my arms. "Get the elevator, Britt! Get it *now*!"

Justin

The suite had two bedrooms and was big enough for both Dex and me. Dex took the smaller bedroom. I'd been beat, and drunk, when we arrived. I fell into bed and passed out.

The next morning, Dex was up and eating a champagne breakfast at the breakfast nook table by the windows. His laptop was open. He was hard at work, sipping his orange juice and distractedly taking bites of scrambled eggs in between. His brows were knitted in concentration.

The smell and sight of food made my stomach lurch. I poured myself a cup of coffee from the carafe in front of Dex.

"What took you so long, sleepyhead? We have work to do." He was annoyingly chipper.

I scowled at him. My head pounded and the light was too bright. Not to mention there was an ache where my heart used to be and my stomach burned with anger.

Dex kicked a chair out for me. "Take a seat, Sunshine." He laughed when I fell into it and put my head in my hand.

"Since you are determined not to see the advantage of Lala carrying your baby—"

"I'm going to divorce her." I'd been thinking it through in my drunken stupor all night. It was the right thing to do for both of us. Time to set her free. But it was the first time I'd said it out loud. It sounded cold and final and unsettled my stomach even more.

"Of course you are," Dex said. "We've known that from the beginning."

I shook my head, which was a mistake. It pounded loud and painfully. I muttered beneath my breath. "No, I mean, really. Not in a year. Not on our anniversary. As soon as we catch this thief. I emailed Harry before I even got out of bed. Told him to look over our postnup and be ready to strike as soon as we've completed our mission down here."

Dex shrugged. "Whatever." He grinned and said with a high degree of sarcasm, "At least you made the decision with a clear head." He pushed a bottle of acetaminophen toward me. "Take two."

I popped two pills and eyed him cautiously. "You're not upset?"

"It's not my life." He was absolutely unperturbed. "My cousin has already gotten what she apparently wanted, and schemed deviously for—an heir to a billionaire's fortune and eighteen to twenty years of generous child support ahead of her. I'm sure she'll get a good lawyer.

"Have you seen the videos of her announcing the pregnancy at your birthday party? My mom already posted one on all her social media sites."

I glared at him.

"Your mom looked happy." Dex was rubbing it in intentionally. "Enjoy your few minutes of being the favorite son. Before you dash her hopes and blow your little family apart, you might consider this—there is no legal right of visitation for grandparents. Lala could legally keep them from seeing their first grandchild. And you would become such a dog in their eyes."

"You're enjoying this." I took a gulp of black coffee.

"Being the voice of reason?" He shook his head. "It's what I live for. Now, do you want to know what I've found out about your real bride?"

"Could you push those eggs farther away? They make me want to throw up."

He shoved them aside without looking at them. "Her name is Macy Long. Well, as far as I can tell. She has about a hundred aliases and false identities. And that's an approximation, not an exaggeration."

"Am I supposed to be impressed?" I was in a foul mood.

"You should be," Dex said. "I know where she lives." He let that revelation hang in the air so I could grasp its importance. Dex had a flair for the dramatic. "Now, drink your coffee and get your head out of your ass. We have some surveillance to do."

I would have shaken my head again, but I'd already learned my lesson. Instead, I took a slow, deep breath. "I have a highly paid PI to do the grunt work for us. Text me what you've got. We'll put his crack team on it. We have better things to do with our time. Like set up a sting. Our file of crackpots is ready to go if we need it?"

Dex looked disappointed about not getting to play PI. He nodded and sent me a text. "Yeah. Hate to break it to you, but you attract a lot of nutcases and women with odd fantasies and weird conspiracy theories. There are at least half a dozen who claim they're having your baby. At least three of them claim you used aliens to impregnate them."

"It's my animal magnetism and winning personality." I rolled my eyes. "I think I game with a few of those psychos online."

"Dude, you got to be more discriminating." Dex laughed.

"I used to be desperate." I downed half a cup of black coffee and grimaced. "We have any energy drinks around here?"

"In the not-so-mini fridge in this place." He hitched a thumb toward it.

I went to the fridge, grabbed one, and popped the top. One of the great things about having money— buying crap from the mini fridge didn't make me wince quite so badly anymore. Dex's text came in. I sent

Dex's info to my guy. "What have you got on our thief? We need to figure out her MO and her weaknesses."

I laughed bitterly. "Oh, wait. We know her weakness, or at least her favorite marks—desperate, geeky rich guys who win cash at the tables. And carry it around for easy lifting."

I knew the answer to the question I was about to ask, but I went ahead with it anyway. "How's your blackjack?"

He shook his head. "I count cards better than you do. How much do you want me to win?"

"Enough to attract our girl. Not enough to draw attention and get thrown out of the casinos. I'll front you the money. But first, we need to plan this out carefully." I studied him. "And pretty you up."

Dex rolled his eyes, looking put out. "Ah, shit, Justin. Lala has rubbed off on you."

Just then my phone buzzed. I had a text from Kay. It was a picture of her and Data. All dolled up and wearing matching rhinestone collars and pink bows. And the message—*From our new Doggy and Me collection. You can try to take the dog from the girl. But you can't take the girl out of the dog.*

I cursed to myself.

"What?" Dex asked.

I handed him the phone. "How did she get my dog back? Ophie took her to a dog sitter. We have to hurry."

Dex broke out laughing.

CHAPTER FIVE

Kayla

On Monday, Magda and the part-time maid came in to do a thorough post-birthday party cleaning. Ophie's fake email supposedly from Britt had gone viral and was all over social media and the gossip news. Even Sunshine Sheri covered it in her typically sensational way—"New bride Kayla Green's marriage has been ill-conceived since the beginning, and so is her child! Our anonymous source, a close insider of Justin's inner circle—"

Ophie, again. Wreaking havoc and in a tempest after I snatched my dog back from her. Oh, and threw up on her. She was probably peeved about that, too. Huh.

"—says that the passion cooled quickly after the impromptu marriage. Realizing she was going to lose Justin, Kayla connived to get pregnant as soon as possible so she could hang on to his money. Sources say that although there was no prenup, the assets Justin came into the marriage with, i.e. the majority of them, are untouchable as long as he hasn't comingled them with Kayla's. Our source says he's been careful to not do exactly that, and, as her marriage has crumbled and she's developed an eye for Lazer Grayson, Kayla has been desperate to find a way to attach herself to Justin's fortune—"

After feeling betrayed by her, Magda had given up watching Sunshine Sheri. But I was a glutton for punishment. Or in this case, a glutton for keeping my finger on the pulse of the gossip. Especially after I'd gotten no response from Jus from my text of Data and me reunited. Did he know what trouble Ophie was causing? Did he care? Or did he still believe the hype?

I was engrossed in the show, my blood pressure going off the charts, I was sure, when Magda came tiptoeing into the room, uncharacteristically tentative.

"Mrs. Justin?"

Magda was old-fashioned. Since Jus had gone, she called me Mrs. Justin exclusively. To her, Mrs. Kayla would mean I was either a widow or a divorcee. And she was still somehow steadfastly refusing to put me into the divorcee category, even though it looked like that was the direction I was heading. At a frighteningly fast pace.

"Yes?" I snapped the TV off out of respect for her.

Magda hesitated, finally coming toward me with her palm outstretched. "Are you missing this? Is this one of your medications? Is it important?"

When she reached me, I looked into her hand and came face to pill with one of my birth control pills. I paled. And went ice cold to the pit of my stomach. Since finding out I was pregnant, I hadn't taken any of my pills. Where had this one come from?

I took it from her tentatively and studied it. "This is one of my birth control pills. Where did you find it?" I couldn't keep from sounding stunned. Surely she wouldn't have been rifling through my stuff.

"It fell out of your little wicker toiletry basket, the one you keep on the bathroom counter by the sink. Veronica found it. When she moved the basket, it fell out." Magda's voice was neutral, but she was studying me intently.

"So that's where it went," I whispered, sudden realization dawning. "Mystery solved!"

On impulse, I jumped up and hugged her. "You found it! You did it! So that's *why* I got pregnant." I squeezed her until I realized I was being inappropriate and let her go.

I punched the air in victory. "I wondered what had happened. Why I got pregnant when I took my pill faithfully."

Her brow knitted.

I laughed. "I was hung—I was taking some pain medication for a headache at the same time I took my pill. I was still half asleep when I popped them in my mouth. I *thought* I heard one drop. But when I looked around, I couldn't find it. So I shrugged it off and chalked it up to my imagination. It must have fallen and lodged in the basket!"

She was still staring at me suspiciously.

"Oh, come, Magda!" I said. "You don't believe the rumors, do you? You don't believe Sunshine Sheri and her ilk? Besides, according to them I flushed my pills!"

I paused, biting my lip as I tried to explain. "I'm a lot of things, but I'm not *totally* stupid. If I was going to get rid of my birth control pills, I certainly wouldn't be dumb enough to toss them in that wicker basket where anyone could find them! For one thing, it's full of holes. They could fall out and give me away." I held the pill up between my thumb and forefinger. "Like this one did."

I shook my head. "I would smuggle the pills out of the penthouse and toss them in the garbage in the lobby, at the very least. Or simply either flush them or wash them down the sink like the gossips are claiming. The pills are tiny. It would be so easy!"

I grabbed her hand. "If I'm the greedy, money-grubbing girl they say I am, and billions were at stake, why would I take any chances of being discovered? Even if I had been dumb enough, or desperate enough, to hide a pill in that basket, I've had plenty of time since to get rid of it. It's almost like it was planted."

I shook my head, still amazed. One mystery solved. "I thought I'd been part of the one percent failure rate. Now I find out it was purely accidental." I cursed myself for being a stupid drunk.

When I returned my gaze to Magda, she was beaming. "I never doubted you, Mrs. Justin. You have to tell Mr. Justin. He's very smart. If he's believing all these rumors, this will bring him to his senses."

I smiled sadly at her, wanting to believe she was right. And thinking he was still too hurt to listen to reason. He hadn't even responded to the text I'd sent him of Data and me looking so adorable in our matching outfits.

Just then my cell phone buzzed. I glanced at it and frowned. "Harry, Justin's lawyer, is downstairs. He wants to come up. I wonder what he wants."

My heart pounded as I buzzed him up, fearing that I knew what he wanted. And it wasn't good. Not at all.

Harry arrived in the penthouse, looking handsome and put together, like always. And smelling characteristically clean and good. But there was something a little off in his usual charming, yet professional demeanor. He seemed, and I hated to say it, nervous and ill at ease.

He was carrying a large legal folder. He made little pretense at small talk, mostly commenting on the unusually hot, dry weather. Yes, yes, a drought, certainly. That was what the weather guys were saying. The hotter than normal weather could continue into *next* summer. Two years of record heat and dry. Seattle was turning brown. Was it really the Emerald City anymore?

"Justin wanted you to have this," he said abruptly. And waved the folder.

Justin

I was holed up in a hotel room I'd rented just for private investigating purposes. My PI, Richard Spize, who went by Dick, naturally, because Dick Spize was a hysterically appropriate name for a private investigator, sat next to me. Sometimes I thought he made it up, like a pen name for an author. I really didn't care one way or the other as long as he got the job done.

We were staring at an open laptop, watching by button camera as Dex trolled for my real little wifey, Macy. He set the bait by playing blackjack game after blackjack game. With my money. The good news was he was good. And winning more than losing. Any losing was done on purpose so the casino wouldn't be wise to him. After all this time, it was odd putting a name to Macy. For so long I'd thought about her as the ID thief, and any other number of expletives.

Dick and I had a team of his go-to colleagues on the floor watching Dex. Dick wore an earpiece. His expression changed from blank to excited in an instant as one of his guys said something to him.

Dick pointed to the edge of the screen. "There. There she is. We've caught her attention."

I found myself oddly dispassionate as I stared into the laptop and watched the woman who'd stolen so much from me. And yet, in an odd way, had given me everything I'd desired. I was the one who'd blown it. I was perfectly willing to take that responsibility. But I wanted her disabled from *ever* getting the truth out. Though, in a weird way, part of me wanted to thank her for bringing things to a head with Kay. If not for the stranger, I would have always wondered whether Kay and I could have had something together. Now I knew.

I turned to Dick. "What do you think?"

Dick studied the laptop. He snapped a screenshot and grinned as he turned to me. "See that expression right there? That smug little look she's wearing. I've seen that expression hundreds of times before. That's what we call falling head, heart, and sinker for our little trap. She's noticed your friend now. She's identified him as her next mark. He's good. He's left just enough cash hanging out of his pockets to catch her eye." Dick laughed. "We'll get her. We've got her now."

My gut clenched. I was ready to confront her. "When do you think she'll make her move?"

Dick was studying the screen again. "Give her a little time to woo him. Thrill of the hunt is part of the game and the high for her. Like a cat playing with a mouse."

I hated to think of myself as her mouse.

"She's watching him to see what he likes before she moves in. She wants to be certain she can charm him. That she knows all she can about him. What he likes to drink. His particular tics. Is he nervous or steady? What kind of woman catches his eye? Our girl Sandra next to him. We already briefed him to play up to her. We want to see if our chameleon will make herself look like Sandra. I believe she will. It's part of her MO.

"Here, let me just switch channels and cue Dex in."

Dex was wearing a wire and a mic.

"Dex, she's spotted you. Don't turn and look, but she's behind you to your left. Flirt with Sandra on your right. Let's force Macy to make a move."

Dick turned back to me. "Don't worry. She has dollar signs in her eyes now. She isn't going to let him get away."

Kayla

I stared at the folder in my hand and back to Harry, my heart in my stomach.

In stark contrast to the first time I'd met Harry, he looked sympathetic. As if he was on my side this time.

"Divorce papers? Again?" I blinked back tears, trying hard not to cry. "What happened to big, paper-serving guy and his black SUV? And shouldn't you say something stunning and erudite like 'You've been served'?" I wiped my eyes with the back of my hand.

Harry looked embarrassed. "These aren't divorce papers. Not yet." He cleared his throat and looked around nervously. "Can we speak in private?"

Which I took to mean not in front of Magda or Veronica, the part-time maid. I led Harry to one of the guest rooms that I'd appropriated for my office, and shut the door.

The room was appointed with a desk, sofa in front of the windows, and chairs.

"Have a seat," I said. "Can I get you something?"

He shook his head. "I'm won't stay long. In fact, I'm not here at all, if you catch my drift. Justin could fire my ass for giving this to you." He waved that intriguing, almost beguiling folder again.

"Now you not only have my attention, but my curiosity as well." I took a seat on the sofa in front of the windows, mostly because it felt like my legs had gone to jelly and were about to give out.

Harry opened the folder and pulled out a familiar envelope.

I gasped.

Harry frowned. "What?"

"I recognize that envelope!" It was the one Jus had caught me with in the closet right after our wedding. The one I'd been so tempted to read. The one that said, *To My Wife Kayla, to be read the day before our divorce.*

So that was what he'd done with it! What was so secret inside it? All the old questions and curiosity surfaced.

"You do?"

I explained.

Harry was still frowning. "I didn't realize you'd seen it before. Justin entrusted this to me with instructions that I was to give it to you the day before your divorce became final."

My heart did a nosedive for my stomach. I went totally cold to the core.

"Yes, I know. It says so on the envelope. Is our divorce *that* imminent, then?" I could barely get the words out. "Don't I have to sign something or something?"

Harry smiled kindly. "Yes, you do. And no, it isn't *that* imminent. But it's coming. Justin has asked me to prepare the paperwork. He's prepared to pay you the agreed-upon sum, but he no longer requires your services for the duration of the contract."

I nodded, trying to swallow the lump in my throat. "And the baby?"

Harry sat next to me on the sofa, after all. "I recommend getting your own lawyer now that you have a child to consider in the dissolution."

I nodded again.

Harry took my hand and squeezed it. "But that's not why I've come. As Justin's good friend, I've seen how good you've been for him. I don't believe what I've seen and heard from the media. It doesn't ring true with what I know about you. From the beginning, you didn't want his money. And while having money can turn a person's head, I don't think that's what's going on with you."

He pressed the letter into my hand. "As Justin's friend, not his lawyer, I'm giving you this letter." He smiled regretfully. "As his lawyer, he could can my ass and have me disbarred. Regardless, I think you need to read this."

I stared at the letter in my hand. "Do you know what this says?"

He shook his head. "I haven't read it, no. But I know it's important for you to have." He stood suddenly.

I looked up at Harry. "Thank you." I bit my lip. I didn't know what to say. "I won't tell him if you won't."

"I'll show myself out."

CHAPTER SIX

Justin

I was impatient. Eager to bring Macy in before she had a chance to get away. Dick and I watched as she hit on Dex. Just as Dick had predicted, she'd morphed into a Sandy clone, even adopting a similar style of dress.

"I wonder whose credit card she used to buy that outfit," I said to Dick. I remembered she'd stolen Kay's and used it to buy the outfit she wore to seduce me. It was sick. She was sick.

But I was impressed with Dex's flirting skills. He was becoming almost suave. And he was throwing my money around like it was nothing.

Dick leaned forward, concentrating on the surveillance feed. "Watch your drink, buddy. We know she likes roofies."

Dex had been warned. There was no antidote for roofies. Unaided by alcohol, it lasted in the system from eight to twelve hours. Taken with alcohol, it could last for as long as thirty-six. Dex was drinking moderately. From what we'd gleaned from her record, Macy was a skilled pickpocket. Which meant she was good at sleight of hand. It would have been easy for her to slip a roofie in Dex's drink without his knowledge. Like she'd done to me.

On our feed, Dex was offering to buy Macy dinner.

"Oh, crap! He's going to draw this out." I banged my fist on the table.

Dick raised one eyebrow. "He's doing fine. He has to win her trust. She's not stupid and she's cautious. She's not going anywhere private with him until she decides he's not a threat and she has the upper hand."

Kayla

Long after Harry had gone, I sat in my office with the envelope trembling in my hand, staring at Justin's precise engineer's handwriting. Once again, my imagination flew with possibilities. Was Harry right to give me this letter? Was I right to read it? What if it said something incriminating? Or was it simply the instructions on how to extricate myself from Justin's life?

There was only one way to find out. I slid my finger beneath the flap of the greeting card envelope and broke the top open. I was nervous. The edge tore raggedly. My fingers shook as I pulled the card out. It was one of those gushy, terribly romantic cards, all done in shades of pink that Jus couldn't see. Which was sweet and touching in itself. *I'm forever and always yours* was printed on the front. It was one of those cards that you could record a message on. When I opened it, it was Jus singing a line from a love song, followed by him saying, *I love you.*

My eyes clouded with tears. It was so sweet and touching. So Jus. So like the old Jus, anyway. I brushed the tears out of my eyes and tried to read, stopping to wipe them away every few lines. Afraid I was going to drip on the card and blur the beautiful words. Justin's hand was clear and easy to read. His heart was on the page.

Dear Kay,

If you're reading this, it means I've tried to win your love over the past year and lost. I've failed at the one thing that was most important to me. And I'm not used to losing. But I've lost you. Which breaks my heart in ways you'll never understand.

Do you believe in love at first sight? I didn't. Until you walked into that class in college. And stole my heart.

The first time I saw you smile and laugh, I knew you were the girl that was meant for me. All this time since college, when it seemed like our paths would never cross again, I still believed. Still fantasized about you. Dreamed about you. I even started Flash with Riggins partly because I knew it was something you would love. I hoped, dreamed, wished it would somehow bring us together. I even fantasized about hiring you. And made plans to do it.

I hope this doesn't sound too creepy and stalkerish, but yes, I was following you. Not physically. Online. Keeping track of you. And if fate hadn't driven you into my arms and life when it did, I would have hired you away from spending your life dealing with tighty whities. Damn, I was jealous of that company for having you. I was on the verge of having my recruiter go after you, when I went to Reno and you walked into that hotel.

If I have to admit it to myself, it was the chance encounter I'd been dreaming of for too long. That meeting, as you know, went completely awry. I was devastated to think you would use me like it seemed you did. Hurt beyond belief.

But when you walked into Harry's office, and I realized you weren't the one who'd conned me, I felt like fate had just been toying with me. Making me wait until the opportunity was perfect, and even I couldn't mess it up.

So before you go, I want you to know the truth—I was so desperate to keep you that I forced your hand. I forced you into this marriage. After you left Harry's I leaked the news of our marriage to the media. I did it. And I take full responsibility.

I played on your good nature. It was wrong. And I'm paying the price for it. For that, I'm deeply sorry. I don't want to ever force your hand again.

I have, and will always, love you.

Jus

My nose was running. Tears streamed down my cheeks. I was a mess. A total wreck. I made myself get up and grab a tissue from my desk. I wiped my eyes.

Jus had taken a big chance writing a letter like this. What if we'd ended badly and he'd no longer wanted me? I guess he would have had Harry destroy the letter.

I wanted Jus back. This Jus who'd written the letter. But was he gone forever? Had I made him a hardened, bitter guy?

My phone rang, startling me so badly I jumped and put a hand to my heart. Britt was calling. I had to talk to someone so I picked up.

"Hey." I sniffled, hoping she didn't notice as I dabbed at my eyes with the tissue.

"Ophie isn't in the office today," Britt said without preamble. "Word is she left for Reno about half an hour ago. Made some excuse about a business emergency and how Justin needed her. I would have called sooner, but I just found out."

Britt talked so fast and was so agitated, she was hard to understand. "I'm sure she's going after Justin. You have to stop her! Get yourself on a plane and go after her! What are you waiting for? Get your billionaire back!"

Justin

Watching your friend hit on your wife isn't the most thrilling thing under ordinary circumstances. In my case, watching Dex hit on, and be hit on by, Macy was at times boring and tedious. At times infuriating. And sometimes completely hilarious. Dex could be surprisingly charming. Watching him work his moves on Macy, leading her on and playing her, was worth the price of admission. Watching her work him? Embarrassing knowing she'd done it to me.

Dick was used to this kind of work and tedium. He was on his sixth cup of coffee. I would have been jazzed and had a hole in my stomach from the amount he'd drunk. But he seemed alert and perfectly calm and relaxed.

Dex treated Macy to an expensive meal on the money he'd won. As we watched her, Dick and I could almost see the wheels turning in her mind—the more Dex spent, the less she had to steal. But Dex had been good about bragging, repeatedly mentioning he'd won over fifteen thousand at the tables. Why wouldn't he blow some of it to impress a girl?

Dick focused his attention on the screen. "The meal's almost over. I'm sure she's going to drug him. You can tell by her body language she's itching to incapacitate him and grab his dough—

"Ah! There. There! There she goes!" Dick almost came out of his chair as he pointed at the screen. "Atta girl. We got it on camera, Dex. She just dropped a pill in your drink."

Dick whistled low. "She's good. I almost missed it. Watch yourself, man. We don't know where she got these roofies. But they're not coloring your drink and she seems unconcerned that they will. Which means they're foreign." Dick laughed. "Not FDA approved, obviously. Take a fake drink. I'll send my girl over to make a switch."

With clever help from one of Dick's female investigators posing as a waitress, Dex had managed to make it look like he'd had four adult beverages already, while actually having nursed maybe one full one.

"Mallory, baby, swoop in and change out our boy's drink, will you, honey? And save it for the lab." Dick watched like a nervous dad as Mallory moved in. "Create a distraction to give Mallory cover, Dex. Ah, good job, man!" Dick grinned as Mallory successfully completed the switch. "Great job, Mallory!"

Dick turned to me. "She's the best!"

"That's what I'm paying for."

"Give it twenty minutes, Dex. It will take that long for the drug to act. This kid is a pro. She's timed it to take effect just as you finish dessert. I'll give you the nod and tell you which symptom to fake when. Hang in there!"

Dick leaned back in his chair, put his hands behind his head, and whistled.

"What do we do now?" I asked. His off-key whistling grated on my nerves.

"We wait." He was smugly self-satisfied. "Within the hour, Dex will be bring her back to this room. And then it's up to you. My guys will be in the adjoining room. You'll have a wire. You need us. You call. We'll get you hooked up here in a minute."

He leaned forward, stared at the laptop, and slapped his knee. "Oh, shit! They ordered the Bombe Alaska!" He guffawed. "Of course they did. It's the hotel's signature dessert. You gotta see this, Justin. Watch. They're about to light it on fire."

Kayla

There's no reason to be a billionaire's wife if you can't get what you want in an emergency. What I wanted was a hired jet to take me to Reno as soon as possible. But I had no idea how to get one. I was half-way to calling Andrea, when I stopped myself and called Lazer instead.

"I'll get my highly trained admin on it immediately."

It was reassuring to hear Lazer's calm, confident voice.

"Andrea could handle this," Lazer said. "She's efficient, too."

"No, not Andrea!" I protested. "There's a reason I called you. Andrea is...too close to Ophie. Not that I think she's purposefully feeding her information. But she thinks highly of Ophie and considers her a mentor."

Lazer paused. "Yeah. I have the same suspicions. I'm looking into it, too, Kayla." From Lazer's tone it sounded like I had passed a test. I wasn't an oblivious noob or something. "Have a safe trip. And good luck. I hope Justin comes to his senses."

And so, voila! I was on a plane and on my way to Reno within the hour. I had just enough time to throw a few things in a bag and catch an Uber to the airport. I could have called the car service, but that seemed over the top. And besides, Jus might get wind of it.

I wanted my visit to be a surprise. And I couldn't be too careful.

Justin

I sat in a chair by the window, listening to the air conditioning running while I waited for my "wife" to arrive. Dick had decamped to the adjoining room with several elite, beefy, security-detail-type members of his crew.

Dex was now feigning the full array of symptoms, acting the part of a roofied mark, leading our thief right to me. He was on his way to "his" room with Macy. Where her plan was that he could pass out thinking he was going to get lucky. And she could steal his hard-won money without having to compromise herself. At least, that was what it appeared to Dick and me.

Lucky her. She was in for a surprise! Her husband was waiting for her. This was going to be some fun fireworks.

There was drunken laughter in the hall. Footsteps stopped just outside the hotel room door. The click of the lock flipping.

My heart pounded in my ears. The door opened.

Dex stood back. "Ladies first!" He handed her in.

At first, she didn't see me. Which had been the plan. She was too busy laughing with Dex, trying to put him at ease. Clearly, she was a seasoned pro.

"Come on, baby," she cooed to him. "Don't be shy! You geek boys are always so sweetly timid. Come on in and have some fun with me. I'll make a man out of you!"

She laughed, looked up, and saw me sitting in the dimly lit room.

"Another time," Dex said, completely soberly as he snatched her purse off her shoulder.

"Hey!" she screamed at him.

He gave her a gentle shove into the room and backed out the door, shutting it and barring it behind him.

I knew the minute she recognized me. Her eyes went wide. She swung around and tried the door, but Dick had it barricaded from the outside. She wasn't escaping. And, with luck, Dex had just disarmed her of any weapons.

She pounded on the door. When that didn't work, she turned around to face me. "You! What do *you* want?"

If Dick hadn't been so thorough, I might have been worried that she had a weapon. Even without one, she was dangerous.

"The question is—what do *you* want?" My voice was surprisingly calm. "Have a seat. I'm not here to hurt you."

"Thank you. I'd rather stand." Her tone was defiant, full of false bravado. Her eyes were wild. She was trying to buy enough time to assess the situation and talk herself out of this one.

"Suit yourself." I shrugged. "You've been sending me messages. You wanted to talk. So talk."

Her eyes narrowed. "And this is how you arranged it? Kidnapped me?"

"Kidnapped? You came back to the room voluntarily with my roommate."

"So what do you want?" She changed course, suddenly putting a purr in her voice.

More flies with honey? Was that her new strategy?

"Answers," I said. "I have some ideas about the last time we were together. But I'd very much appreciate it if you would fill in the blanks."

"Oh, you would?" She laughed and took a seat on the bed across from me. "I know who you are. A little late, but I figured it out. You really are a cutie pie." She leaned forward to touch me.

I leaned away from her. "Last time we met, you drugged me. Like you just attempted to do to my friend."

"Drugged you? Oh, that? Is that what you're calling it now? That was purely consensual. You asked for it. Don't you remember, baby? How comforting I was? You appreciated it well enough then.

"If only I'd realized that night that you were more than just a broke college kid with a knack for playing blackjack. You count cards, don't you?" She shook her finger at me. "That will get you banned. Ah, well. Lost opportunities, right?"

I didn't answer.

"You wanted something to ease your pain. You were upset that the Kayla bitch stood you up. Cruel woman. Leading you on like that.

"You were drunk. Very drunk. So you probably don't remember me saying I could give you something to dull the heartache. I put it in your drink. With your permission. You practically begged me. You certainly saw me. You even paid me a little something for my trouble."

"*You* broke my heart," I said, trying to hold back the bitterness.

"Did I? Ain't that sweet? I didn't realize you were that into me."

I shook my head. She was a piece of work. "You had Kay's phone. It was in her purse when you stole it. You were the one who replied to my texts. So, in a sense, *you* stood me up. You certainly set me up."

She laughed. "You're a regular card, Justin. I *found* her purse."

When she smiled, she revealed slightly stained teeth. The bottom ones were crooked and one had a small chip. And she had to be a good ten years older than Kay. A cheap imitation. Tonight, when she wasn't trying to be Kay, I found her repulsive.

"And returned it like a Good Samaritan by stashing it in a potted plant in the lobby after stripping it of her credit cards and cash?" I caught a whiff of her perfume. It brought back snatches of memories from that night.

I had been very drunk by the time she approached me. She was telling the truth about that. Never drink to get over a woman. I had to have been smashed not to have seen, and cared about, the stark differences between her and Kay. Her hardness and Kay's gentle sweetness.

I'd already admitted too much. I had to get what I wanted from her without admitting to participating in a wedding ceremony with her. I didn't want anything either on, or off, the record. Nothing she could use against me.

Fortunately, I hadn't confessed to anything essential. Hell, Kay could have "stood me up" and changed her mind later and married me. I caught myself from saying more. And reminded myself to proceed with caution. "Tell me more. Fill in the gaps in my memory. Why did you choose me?"

"What's it worth to you?"

"I'll make it worth your while." I kept my tone even and fought to keep my anger under control. I didn't believe in hurting women, but I could hardly stand to look at her. And yet I felt an odd well of sympathy for her. In her own way, she was pathetic and in need of help.

"I'd seen you around the hotel before. Several times. I wanted to get to know you. Is that so wrong? You're cute."

I scowled at her.

She laughed. "And modest. You don't believe me. You don't believe in your appeal." She shook her head. "That makes you even hotter."

I ignored her come-on. "So you'd pegged me for a good mark."

"You're too cynical for someone so young. You looked like you'd be fun to hang with. That's all."

"And you got lucky. I texted Kay. You had her purse and phone and took advantage of the situation," I said, filling in the blanks.

She flipped her hair off her shoulder. "Not at all. You'd won big at the tables earlier that evening. You had plenty of cash on you and were reckless. Flashing it around. I figured you could show a girl a good time."

I remembered that much. "You're not telling me anything I don't know."

She shook her finger at me again. "Never flash that kind of cash around. I figured I should get close and warn you. You never know who will be watching and want to take it away from you."

"Someone like you?" I watched her carefully.

"Me?" She shook her head. "You really *don't* remember. You *gave* me the money. You *did*. For the fun of the evening. And making your dreams come true. Fulfilling your fantasy. I never stole it. I never stole anything in my life."

I lifted an eyebrow.

She shrugged. "Maybe years ago. But not *your* money. That was a gift. You can't hang stealing on me. Or kidnapping. Or drugging you against your will. That's all fiction. You don't even remember."

"So fill me in." I paused, afraid to continue. "*How* did you fulfill my fantasies?"

"Oh, baby. What I gave you made you higher than a kite. High, you were completely hilarious. Cute. Sweet. Indignant. Insecure. Upset. What could I do but help you out? I'd be a hard woman if I didn't.

"You said Kayla was the only girl for you. The girl you were destined to marry. But she'd never have you. You said you were rich. In retrospect, I should have paid more attention and really listened to what you were saying. But you flashed some cash you'd won at the tables. Lots of cash. And I thought that's what you meant by rich. I had no idea you were a billionaire. You *are* a billionaire, aren't you, Justin?"

I shrugged. "One of Seattle's youngest."

She smiled again, this time regretfully. "See? If I'd known that, I would have signed my own name on the marriage license."

She shook her head and sighed. "Anyway, Kayla had just stood you up, proving your point—she didn't want you. You aren't her type, evidently. Not like your friend Lazer Grayson. But then, he's a hottie, isn't he?"

I clenched my jaw and my fists. She was baiting me. She wanted me to come out of my chair and hurt her. Presumably so she could sue me and get some of my cash she'd missed out on the first time around. "Don't believe everything you hear from the tabloids," I said, calmly. In business, I could bluff with the best of them. "You were saying?"

Her eyes flashed with a spark of anger. She lifted her chin, clearly frustrated. She'd underestimated the sober version of me.

"I was looking for a lark, an adventure. I like the thrill of getting away with as much as I can. You might call me a prankster. A thrill-seeker," she said, putting the purr back in her voice. She didn't know how to handle me. She was fishing for something that worked.

"So I thought up a plan. I told you I could fix it so she married you. Well, more accurately, I could make it *look* like she'd married you. I'm not a *complete* miracle worker, after all." She looked around the room, suddenly nervous. "Are we all alone?"

I held my hands out, palms up. "Completely."

"I don't trust you. Not after you just pulled a sting on me." She pouted.

"I guess we're even, then," I said. "I don't trust *you*, either. But I want to hear your side of the story. Proceed."

She looked around again, maybe hoping the cavalry might arrive out of the blue—who knew what was going through her mind—and shrugged. "There isn't much more to tell. You described Kayla to me in detail. How she acted, her mannerisms and the like. And I made myself look as much like her as I could.

"We went to an all-night wedding chapel. I'd found her purse. I had her driver's license. They don't check too closely anyway, at that chapel. If a couple wants to get married, who are they to interfere? So long as they get their money, they're happy.

"Just in case, I practiced her signature so it looked like a good fake."

"It didn't take much practice," I said. "According to your record, you're a master forger."

She smiled, ignoring my comment. "You were out of it. I had to do most of the talking and convincing. I paid for the basic package with money out of your wallet. I pretended to be her. Said the vows. Promised to love you until death do us part. As her, of course. Forged her name on the license and handed it to you. There. You married her. See? Easy.

"It was a great joke. A real thrill to get away with faking a marriage. You were so high that I had to help you back to your room. See, as your new wife I was concerned about you like that. Then you gave me your winnings for my trouble. And I went on my way."

"No sex?" I asked.

"What do you think I am? A whore? A rapist? I don't do comatose guys!" She puffed up, indignant.

I almost sagged with relief. I believed she was being truthful on that point.

"That's a nice story," I said. "Do you tell it at bedtime?"

Her eyes narrowed. "You don't believe me?"

"Why should I? Especially when the woman I really married has been my wife almost three months."

"Ha!" She let out a laugh that was almost a cackle. "So I did grant your wish! I'm better than I thought. I deserve a bonus. But the truth is, you aren't married to her. And probably not to me, either. Unfortunately. Because I'd like to be a billionaire's wife. I really would."

"I bet you would."

We stared at each other. It was clear neither of us were going to change our story. It was my word against hers. To be honest, both stories sounded implausible. But I was the more reliable witness. With better references and a bigger fan club. And Kay, if she didn't back out of her story.

I came directly to the point. "Why have you been sending me texts trying to extort money from me?"

Her eyebrows shot up. She was overacting. "I wasn't trying to extort *anything* from you. I was just trying to warn you. You aren't really married to that girl. Maybe you think you are, but you aren't.

"I don't know what you told her. But she's taking advantage of you. Now that I know who you are, I see

why. It's your money she wants. And who wouldn't?"
She paused to study me again.

"I can get you out of your marriage. I mean, you had
to have married without a prenup." She pointed between her and me. "*We* didn't have a prenup. You got a
lot of money you stand to lose. I could come in and tes-
tify that your so-called marriage wasn't legal. None of
it. Because I knowingly signed a fake name. Even in
Nevada that won't stand up. Then you'd be free and
clear. No money lost. Long as you don't press charges
against me. And I make a little something, I'm good."

I sighed. I wasn't about to tell her the real arrangement Kay and I had. "There are all kinds of crazies in
this world and you're just another one of them. Do you
know how many threats I get? How many girls claim
they've slept with me? Or secretly married me? I have a
file full. In fact, some of them might even leak to the
press."

I took a deep breath. "Let me tell you a story, a true
story. There is a girl. Her name is Macy. She stole my
wife's purse, her phone, her credit cards, and her iden-
tity. And charged an ungodly sum to them that I had to
pay off. All that is irrefutable. The evidence has been
turned over to the police. This girl, Macy, has a long
history of stealing identities. She'll probably to go to
prison when the prosecutor gets through with her.

"But it's all white-collar crimes. Nothing violent.
Nothing threatening. It could go worse for her if we
decided to turn over the drugged drink that's now in
our lab's possession. Or I decide to press charges for
drugging me."

I leaned forward and stared deep into her eyes. "Look. In a way, you did me a favor. I'm willing to forget about the drugging and that ten thousand dollars you took from me. And I will. As long as you never mention this marriage shit again. No more threats."

Her eyes flashed with anger again. "Am I being held prisoner here?"

I indicated the door. "You're free to go anytime. Have been the entire time." I held out my hand. "But first, I want my friend's money back."

Her eyes were fierce, but there was fear behind it. She handed over ten thousand dollars. I counted it. I held out my hand again and wagged my fingers at her. "There's more."

She handed me another thousand. She had another four or five of Dex's money. But what the hell? I let her have it as a goodwill gesture.

Our eyes met. She knew she wasn't fooling me. She could consider it hush money. I didn't care.

"Are we done here?" she said.

CHAPTER SEVEN

Kayla

I was on my way from the Reno airport to the hotel Justin always stayed at when I got a call from Britt.

"Kayla, you won't believe this." She was excited. "I just saw a promo for Sunshine Sheri's show tomorrow. She's doing an entire show on deluded, nutcase women who make up crazy stories about celebrities and wealthy men. Things like how they slept with them and had their baby. Totally untrue crap that some of the actually believe.

"And get this—she said she has an entire file on crazy claims made against Lazer Grayson and Justin! Sheri's promo piece says there are at least a dozen women who've tried to blackmail Justin saying he secretly married them!

"And then I saw a teaser for the nightly news with the same theme—crazy women who make outrageous claims to get money from rich men."

My heart stopped for a second. Until the full implication set in. What was Justin up to?

Justin

Dick's team tailed Macy when she left. The police picked her up and arrested her in the lobby before she could escape. His guys called Dick and gave him the news. There were high fives all around.

As Dick's team cleaned up and prepared to leave, Dex pulled me aside. "The second part of our plan is in full swing. Our leak to the news is going as planned. The truth has been completely obfuscated, muddled, and obliterated. Even the major news shows are picking up the stories of crazy allegations that have been made against wealthy guys by gold-digging women. If Macy ever tries it, no one will believe her."

I nodded. "Good."

Dex slapped me on the back. "Good job tonight."

"Good job you! You were a star," I said to him.

He grinned. "I live for this kind of shit. It's the ultimate prank. Crap, it gives me a thrill." He took a deep breath. "I'm too wound up to sleep. I'm going to hit the casino and celebrate."

"Don't get too carried away," I warned him. "Keep your guard up and don't get cocky, kid."

"Never!" he said.

I was beat and needed time to myself. I left Dick's team to finish up and went back to the suite.

I slipped inside and closed the door with my back to the body of the room. I caught a whiff of perfume. My heart stopped. "Kay?"

I spun around.

Ophie was sitting on the sofa. My heart fell. Shit. What was *she* doing here?

"Ophie?" I frowned.

She was wearing an outfit that had the Flashionista style to it. It should have been chic. On Kay, it would have looked fantastic. On Ophie it made her look both like a little girl playing grownup and a dowdy old lady at the same time. She'd died her hair blond and had it cut in a style that was eerily similar to Kay's.

"What are you doing here?" And how did she get in?

She stood up and smoothed her skirt. "Riggins sent me down to check on you. He thought you'd need my assistance while you're here. I thought it was a good idea to have someone loyal to you nearby. You were so upset when you left.

"Besides, I couldn't refuse a direct order from Riggins. Not without giving away that you're here on personal business. He didn't seem to know what was really going on. I figured you wanted it that way. Anyway, you and I can get some work done while you get yourself together after..."

She walked to the fridge. "You look tired." She opened the fridge door and pulled out an energy drink. She walked over to me, popped the top of the drink, and handed it to me. "Your favorite. Thirsty? You look like you could use it."

She was right. I was parched. I downed half the can in a single gulp. "It's late. You should get back to your room."

"I will. In a few minutes. First, let me brief you about what's going on at the office." She took my hand and pulled me to the sofa.

Kayla

"Look. Here's my license." I slapped it on the counter at the hotel registration desk. "I'm Kayla Green. Justin Green's wife. I know he's staying in a suite here. Just give me a key to his room and I'll be on my way."

The guy behind the counter looked at me suspiciously as he slid the license to him. Thank goodness I'd taken Magda's advice and changed my name months ago.

"I'll have to call Mr. Green to verify—"

I grabbed his arm. "Don't bother Justin." I leaned forward and whispered to the clerk, "I'm trying to surprise him. Run the license. Or one of my credit cards." I let go of his arm and pulled a credit card from my purse. "You'll see they're legit. And I look just like the picture on the license. It was only taken a few months ago."

I looked him in the eye and he gave in and made me a key.

I handed him a hundred-dollar bill for his trouble. "Thank you."

Justin

Ophie talked and talked until I started to feel thick-headed and dull. Drunk. I couldn't form words properly. I was having trouble talking.

"Sorry, Jus!" Ophie said. "You look exhausted. And I'm boring you. I should leave." She stood.

I stood to see her out and my legs nearly gave out. My motor skills were off. My muscles didn't want to work.

"Oh, you really are dead on your feet." Ophie put her arm around my waist and leaned her head on my shoulder. "Lean on me. I'll help you to bed."

I tried to form the words to protest, but none came out. I found myself leaning on her.

With her help, I staggered into the bedroom. She managed to open the bed and I fell into it.

"Here. Let me help you get undressed before I leave." She pulled off my shoes and began tugging on my jeans.

Kayla

So in the crazy way of the world, I had to show more ID to get a key to my husband's hotel room than the ID thief had to marry him in the first place. It had been no problem for her to marry him as me. But a big deal for me to get a key. If any of the porters had seen the size of the tip I'd given the clerk at reception, I would have been swarmed. But I preferred to wheel my own suitcase up.

As I got in the elevator, my pulse went crazy rapid, beating so loud it pounded in my ears. What, exactly, was I going to say to Jus? I'm here to save you from dear Ophelia? Ophie's the devil disguised as an efficient administrative assistant?

I had no idea, really. But I kept my eyes open for her, expecting to run into her at every turn.

I found my way to Justin's room with no problem. He was in the top-floor executive suite, naturally. The boy did love his penthouses. I paused just for a second outside the door of his room, screwing up my courage and trying to calm my nerves. I took a deep, supposedly calming breath, and slid my keycard in the reader, crossing my fingers that he hadn't latched the dead-bolt.

Sometimes fate smiles on you and gives you your wish. I got mine—no deadbolt. The door swung open. I wheeled my suitcase in and stepped into an empty room. It was a suite, though, with two bedrooms. Convenient for me if we still weren't going to act like man and "wife."

I sniffed, catching a trace of a perfume suspiciously like mine. A woman's purse sat on the coffee table next to an open can of energy drink, Justin's favorite. The air conditioning hummed. But not loud enough to cover the sounds of bed pounding and headboard banging coming from the bedroom.

That was when rage sent me over the edge of reason. Eric had screwed around on me and got away with it. In hindsight, because although I thought I loved him, I really hadn't. But Jus was another case altogether. He was not going to get away with making a fool out of me.

I let go of my suitcase handle, grabbed a nice handy, heavy bookend for defense, and stormed the bedroom. I banged the door open to find a newly blond Ophie, dressed only in a thong panty and see-through bra, a set I'd seen recently featured on Flash, on top of Jus, straddling him, ineptly trying to ride him. Or maybe she was just trying to undress him. It was hard to tell from my angle. His shirt was on and mostly unbuttoned and falling away from his chest and shoulders. Ophie's head was down as she fumbled with something. The last button on his shirt?

With the blond hair, it took me a second to recognize her. For an instant I thought he'd hooked up with his real wife, the ID thief. That's how much Ophie was trying to imitate me. A cheap imitation, I might add.

Justin's jeans were in a pile on the floor next to his shoes. Ophie's clothes were laid out neatly over the back of a chair. Jus still had his socks and boxers on. One of the funny, cute pairs of shorts I'd bought for him in Italy.

Okay! This looked bad. And almost funny at the same time. Obviously, Ophie didn't have the necessary experience undressing drunk guys to be proficient at it. Or having sex with them. I had way too much and could have given her a lesson. But I'd never had sex with a guy so drunk he was practically comatose. That was bad news all around. What was she trying to do with Jus? Rape him or frame him?

Rage really can blind a person. I was so angry and hurt that I could have committed a crime of passion right then. And I'm normally nonviolent.

But, as I'd learned, appearances can be deceiving. I wasn't about to overreact like Jus had. And believe me, this situation was much more damning than a robed hug with a fully dressed Lazer.

Poor, inept Ophie. Generally, if you were going to do it on top, you took your panties off. Especially if you were a beginner. Though getting around a thong wasn't a problem, Jus still had his shorts on. And it didn't look like anything was peeking out, if you know what I mean.

"Justin Arnold Green! What are you doing with that woman?"

Okay, so I sounded more like his mom than his outraged wife who'd just caught him with a lover.

Ophie froze.

Jus came out of his passed-out state just enough to lift his head groggily and stare at me with unfocused eyes. "Kay?"

And then it hit me. *Crap, Jus! Not again.*

Ophie turned and looked at me with a panicked expression. Like I might throw up on her again. Oh, I had worse in mind.

Fury gave me the strength of a dozen pregnant, wronged, fake wives. I didn't see straight. And I certainly didn't think. I strode to the bed, grabbed Ophie by the hair, and pulled her off my guy.

She screamed as I dragged her by the hair, ready to pull it out by its bleached blond roots if necessary, off Jus and onto the floor.

"Get up, bitch!" I grabbed her arm, the weighty bookend still in my other hand. Hey, I could club left-handed if I had to. "What did you do to him? What did you give him?"

"Nothing!" she screeched.

"Liar. You drugged him, you bitch!" I pulled her to her feet and dragged her to the door of the suite. "What did you slip him?"

"Nothing! Let go of me."

I tossed her nearly naked ass into the hall, latching the lock and the deadbolt behind her. If she wasn't going to cooperate, neither was I.

She pounded on the door, begging to be let back in.

I ignored her and strode back to the bedroom and sat gently on the bed next to Jus.

He leaned up on his elbows, weak and unsteady as he tried to focus on me. "This isn't what it looks like, Kay. You have to believe me."

Well, that was what I thought he was trying to say, anyway. His words were slurred and choppy, unformed, as if his tongue was thick and wasn't working properly.

"Oh, I know it." I put a hand to his cheek. "Things aren't always what they seem, Jus. Just remember that when you come out of this. If you can. You have a nasty habit of getting roofied. I'm pretty sure that's what Ophie did. Didn't your mom ever tell you not to take an open drink from someone? What did she give you?"

He frowned, clearly trying to think. It wasn't like Jus to have trouble thinking or remembering. "Energy drink?" he finally got out.

I nodded. "I thought so." I squeezed his arm. "Lie down. I'm going to get help."

I grabbed my cell phone and called 911. When they picked up, I explained the situation in a surprisingly calm voice. "There's a deranged nearly naked woman in the hall outside my husband's hotel room. I think she drugged him. He should probably be checked out and tested for roofies.

"When the police get here, there's an energy drink can on the coffee table. They should test it for drugs, too."

CHAPTER EIGHT

Kayla

The police arrived and arrested Ophie. I was against giving her her clothes. But I didn't fight it when one of the officers retrieved them from the suite.

I rode with Jus in the ambulance to the hospital, holding his hand like the good fake wife I was. The doctors wanted to check him out and observe him while they waited for the results from the energy drink. Or Ophie confessed to what she'd given him.

Jus babbled on about always loving me. I wondered, I hoped, the old Jus was back. But when he came back to his right senses? Who knew?

I held his hand and put a finger to his lips to shush him. Even though he was nearly unintelligible, I didn't want him saying anything he might regret. Outing us at this point, after so much effort to make our marriage look real, would make the whole charade futile.

"You are so not going to remember this." I brushed the hair off his forehead.

The paramedic riding with us smiled.

I texted Dex with a brief explanation and asked him to meet us at the hospital. He arrived shortly after they took Jus back to be examined. It was either late night or early morning depending on your point of view and whether you were a glass-half-empty or glass-half-full kind of person. We got coffee in the hospital cafeteria.

"What the hell are you doing in town and what happened?" Dex asked when we were seated with our coffee. "When I left Justin, he was going back to the suite to go to bed. And then suddenly all hell breaks loose."

He shook his head. "This better be good. I was on a winning streak. I had to leave a lucrative game of craps to get here."

"Poor baby." I had zero sympathy for him. "When you left him from doing what?"

"I asked first," Dex said with his impish smile.

"We aren't going to play *that* old game, are we?"

He raised both eyebrows and waited. As kids, we were always trying to get the best of each other and make the other go first.

"Fine," I said, not in the mood to play games. "Britt called me this morning to tell me Ophie had flown down here and I'd better get my butt down here and stop her from causing more trouble—"

"You're talking to Britt now?" He raised an eyebrow. "After she sent the email congratulating you on trapping Justin with a baby?"

"You heard about that?" I wrapped my hands around my coffee cup, trying to soak up some warmth. It was cool inside in the air conditioning. Or maybe I was just cold in my soul. Of course Dex knew about the email. He knew everything.

"Justin told me everything—about the email and walking in on you and Lazer."

I frowned. "Everything from his point of view, I imagine."

"Yeah," Dex said. "But I defended you. And Britt. I gave him all the logical reasons Britt wouldn't have sent that email. It just didn't make sense." He detailed them for me.

"Your logic is impeccable." I smiled just a little. Dex was always right on target. "She didn't. Ophie did."

"Why doesn't that surprise me?" He took a sip of coffee and looked deep in thought for a minute.

I explained what had really happened. How Ophie had overheard Britt and me at lunch that day. And then sent the email from Britt's work computer. How she'd set Lazer and me up time and time again. And how Jus had walked in on something totally innocent.

"I admit that I was attracted to Lazer in the beginning. I mean, my 'marriage' to Jus was sudden and kind of sprung on me."

I lowered my voice and leaned close to Dex so no one else could hear. "It was just a business arrangement.

And I'm human. But I fell in love with Jus. It's almost impossible not to."

I sighed. "What hurts so much is that he jumped to conclusions. Yes, I know from the outside it looked bad. But he knows me. He knew how I felt about him. Yet he didn't trust me. He didn't hear me out. He just walked away." I blinked back a tear.

"You told Lazer you'd always love him," Dex pointed out. "That's more than a little condemning. Not easy for any guy to hear."

I nodded. "I was telling Lazer that, yes. But I wasn't finished. I was telling him I'd always love him like a friend or a brother. But Jus was the guy I'd always love. Hearing the whole thing makes all the difference."

Dex nodded. "Justin has always been insecure where you're concerned. Can you blame him?"

I took a deep breath. "If he and I are ever going to stand a chance together, he has to get over it. Looked at in a different light, he's way above me now, isn't he? With all his money? And the way I've fixed him up, he's hot. Women want him." My laugh was bitter. I paused, debating with myself for a second. "Jus is going to divorce me."

"That's been a given since the beginning," Dex said in his typical deadpan tone.

"No. I mean *now*." I swallowed hard. "Harry came to see me and warn me. It was nice of Harry. He wanted to give me time to get a good lawyer. For the baby." I kept the rest of what Harry had done for me secret, as he'd requested. "Don't tell Jus."

"Wouldn't dare."

"Your turn," I said. "What is going on here in Reno? What have you and Jus been up to?"

His eyes lit up and his voice grew excited as Dex filled me in.

"You caught her?" I paused, trying to figure out my warring emotions. "I'm relieved, of course. On the other hand, if she really is silenced, there's no reason for Jus not to proceed with the divorce now. Like Harry said he would."

I thought about the letter again. But that was the old Jus who would have done anything to keep me. This Jus, the one who'd walked out on me? I'd come to Reno to stop Ophie from causing more trouble. To talk to Jus and try to get him to see sense. Now, though, circumstances had changed. It was up to him to decide what he wanted to do. Time to set him free. Not that he needed that power from me. He had it all on his own.

"What about tonight? What's all this about Ophie drugging Justin?" Dex asked.

I filled him in on the details.

"You threw her out by her hair?" Dex actually grinned. He found the whole thing incredibly funny. "That's a catfight I'm sorry I missed. Way to go, Lala! I knew you had some good fight in you."

"Well, I caught her riding my husband. What else was I supposed to do?" I shook my head. "See what I mean? My first instinct when I walked in on them wasn't to condemn Jus, but to defend him." I swallowed a lump in my throat.

Dex reached across the table and squeezed my hand. "What are you going to do now?" Dex tilted his head, studying me. "Do you love him?"

"Crazily, I do." I laughed. "Do you remember in college when you told me I should marry him? He was just a scrawny, nerdy kid then." I laughed. "Well, I guess you were right. But times have changed. It's up to him now, not me." I paused. "Any advice for me?"

He shook his head and dropped my hand. "This is all your call, Lala. I'll back you up no matter what you decide. You know that."

I nodded. "I know."

I stared past him out the dark windows, seeing only what was in my mind's eye. It would be daylight soon. Time for a fresh start.

"I think I'll go home." I nodded, more to myself than anything. "Yes, I'll go home."

We sat in silence a second.

"If past history is any indication, Jus won't remember anything of this when he wakes up."

My phone buzzed. I had a text from the doctor. "Jus is going to be fine," I told Dex. "Roofies, as suspected. They're going to keep him for observation while he sleeps it off." I paused. "You'll tell him I was here. And what happened?"

"Yes, absolutely." Dex frowned. "You're leaving now?"

I nodded again. "When Jus finds out what happened, he'll be embarrassed. Maybe ashamed. In shock. He trusted Ophie. He's going to feel betrayed and hurt. I don't need to see that. I have no sympathy for her.

"He needs time to himself to think and sort things out. To figure out what he wants now." I paused again. "*He's* going to have to come back to me. If that's what he wants. I'll be in Seattle. He knows where to find me."

I grabbed my purse and brought up the menu on my phone.

"What are you doing?"

"Calling for a jet home and a ride to the airport." I winked at him. "And as soon as the sun is up, I think I'll call Sunshine Sheri and give her the scoop of the season."

"About what?" Dex asked.

"About Ophie." I laughed darkly. "The news is going to get hold of this story. I may as well get my side out and make an ally out of an enemy."

"You're an evil woman, cuz." He looked at me with admiration when he said it.

I shrugged and laughed, softly. "Aren't I, though?"

I went back to Seattle, picked Data up from Magda, and moved back to my West Seattle apartment in a single suitcase. Partly to make a point to Jus that I didn't give a damn about his money. Partly because I needed time to think.

Enough money made life easier. Too much made it both more luxurious and harder. But cash, by itself, didn't make life wonderful and worth living. Love and people did that. My apartment was warm and homey and, most of all, completely mine. Totally affordable, at least for the time being with the rent paid up for another nine months. And I had enough room for a baby. At least until the baby got a little older.

When Carl saw me coming in wheeling a gigantic suitcase and carrying Data, he rushed out of his office and gave me a hug.

"I saw Sunshine Sheri's show this morning about all the loonies who make up shit about sleeping with billionaires. I'm real sorry about what his assistant did. Looks like you're the hero of the story."

I shrugged modestly. "Sheri did a nice job with the story." I think she'd even redeemed herself with Magda, who asserted she'd never liked Ophie. And would now be watching Sheri's show again.

"She's doing a whole segment on your husband's assistant tomorrow." Carl's gaze took in my huge suitcase. "Didn't work out with the billionaire?" His voice was full of sympathy.

"Hiding from the media attention the story caused," I lied. Well, actually, told a half-truth. The same one I'd told my parents and everyone. "Until it blows over. Jus is out of town cleaning up the fallout and dealing with business. I got homesick rattling around the big penthouse. And tired of the reporters outside the building."

I stroked Data behind her ears and cooed to her before looking back at Carl. "I'd appreciate it if you kept it quiet that I'm back. Unless you want camera crews hanging around here, too."

"Absolutely. Speaking of secrets, are we going to be seeing that big, divorce-paper-serving guy again? 'Cause I can give him the heave-ho next time he shows up here if you want. Or deny that you're here." Carl was hard to fool.

I squeezed his arm. "I hope not." And I meant it. "If he shows up, though, show him in." I let go of his arm.

Carl nodded. "You got it, kid."

Data gave a happy yip.

Carl talked baby talk to her, which was hilarious coming from such a big guy, and scratched her beneath her chin. "By the way, I'll need a pet deposit."

"Charge it to Jus," I said. Well, why not? He owed me for sitting for his dog. Though some might say I'd illegally taken custody of Data.

After parking my suitcase and calling that settling in, I dove headfirst into my duties running Justin's charitable causes. The sample sale and gala was less than two weeks away. It kept me so busy I didn't have a lot of time to dwell on my circumstances.

Jus and I didn't speak or communicate. Every day I expected one of two things to happen—either to be served with a summons to Harry's office to finalize our divorce, or to receive a huge bouquet of flowers and an apology from Jus. Neither came. Each day passed quietly.

I heard through Britt that Jus fired Ophie. Though Jus managed to suppress the exact details of what had happened, the scandal spread through Flash amid a flurry of speculation. People couldn't believe what she'd done. Most people had known or suspected she was in love and obsessed with Jus. But that she would go so *far* was almost beyond belief.

Ophie was charged with various crimes, including assault.

The second-quarter numbers came out, and surprisingly Wall Street responded with a glowing assessment that sent stock prices soaring and made Jus a billionaire several more times over. I thought, cynically, that I deserved a share of the increase. Not that I wanted it. I didn't want anything from Jus except his love and financial support for the baby.

I had the beginning of a baby bump now. I couldn't help thinking Jus would have loved to see it. Maybe he did see it. Maybe he followed me online. Just in case, I posted pictures, hoping he was still keeping track of me.

Justin

I'd screwed up. Bigger than I ever had. Trusted the wrong woman. Didn't believe the right one. By the time I got out of the hospital, talked to the police, gave my statement, finished up some business, and returned to Seattle, Kay had moved out of the penthouse. With my dog. I didn't blame her. I'd expected it.

I didn't need time to think. I knew what I wanted. The same thing I'd always wanted—Kay. And now our baby. I was embarrassed and humiliated. I needed to win her back. I needed to make a grand gesture so she believed I was genuine. And I needed to do it when it was clear I no longer needed her for cover. That I had no ulterior motives.

Business took me out of town for over a week. And that was fine by me. The penthouse was too quiet. Even

Magda had gone silent and sullen. She blamed me for the way things were.

I finally worked up the nerve to open Lazer's present. It was a special limited edition of his game. With a special level where I was the hero who saved the princess Kay. And she showered me with affection. And we lived happily ever after together. So, yeah, that game had been his way of apologizing.

Lazer called while I was in Paris on business.

"I wasn't sure you'd take my call," Lazer said when I picked up.

"To be honest, I should have called you," I said. "I owe you an apology. I jumped to conclusions—"

"Ah, hell, shut up, Justin," Lazer said. "I'm the one calling to apologize. What you walked in on that day was completely innocent, but I'd given you enough reason in the past to take it wrong. I'm a shameless flirt. You know that."

"Really? I hadn't noticed."

Lazer laughed softly. "Look, I'm sorry, Justin—"

"Enough said. Bygones," I said.

"I heard about Ophie," he said.

"Who hasn't?" I sighed. Sunshine Sheri had had a large segment on her show about it.

"Look, I don't want to pile on, but I have to apologize on that front, too. I inadvertently aided Ophie's cause when I lent Kayla my intern Andrea. I meant it as a goodwill gesture to help Kayla out."

Sure he did. He'd been keeping an eye on me and hoping to get closer to Kay. We both knew it. I let it drop.

"Andrea later confessed to me in tears that she felt partly responsible for what had gone on," he said. "She was in awe of Ophie's competence and skill and considered her a mentor. Ophie often asked about me and my schedule. Since Andrea was friends with my OA, and part of my team, she had access to my calendar. She fed it to Ophie, not realizing she was using it to throw Kayla and me together.

"Ophie was obviously trying to set us up. She got lucky that day you walked in on us. That was unfortunate timing. I'd been telling Kayla how happy I was for you two. And she was telling me how much she loved you." He paused. "I don't want to be the reason you two broke up. She loves you. Don't be an idiot about this, Justin. Get her back."

CHAPTER NINE

Kayla

I had to get a new dress for the big sample sale. All those tight dresses from Italy were getting a little too snug in the waist. The few that might have worked I didn't have the heart to wear. Fresh starts and all. So I bought one from Flash. Which seemed appropriate, given the event.

The big sample sale event was on Saturday, September sixth. Which happened to correspond to what would have been our three- month anniversary, or mensiversary, or whatever you wanted to call it. I was glad I had the event to keep me occupied. It was better than dwelling on my sadness and heartache. Better than sitting home crying over what might have been.

Saturday morning I got my hair done and went to the spa and had a manicure and pedicure. Jus hadn't cut my allowance or cancelled my credit cards, so why not?

The evening of the gala, I planned to dress with care. You never knew who would show up at one of these events. Maybe even Jus.

It was wishful thinking, but just in case he did show up, I'd had a mensiversary cake made and decorated with that custom cake topper I'd had made.

Justin

I stared at my reflection in the mirror above the sink in my bathroom, beard clipper poised. A razor on the counter next to the sink. *Grand gesture*, I thought.

From the very beginning Kay had hated this beard. Her one marriage stipulation had been that I would get rid of it. Because of her soft heart, she'd settled for a good trim. The last few weeks I'd been depressed. I hadn't cared about my appearance. Now it was time for more than a trim. If I was going to get the girl back, I needed to do it barefaced. I put the closest guard on the clipper and went to work.

Kayla

We held the sample sale at a local hotel on the water in downtown Seattle. It wasn't far from the Flashionista offices.

People lined up for the sample sale hours early. I had my staff of Flashionista volunteers on hand and ready for our grand opening. Some of them were going to act as cashiers. Some, mostly merch buyers, were going to be fashion consultants to shoppers, and some were personal shoppers for clients who either couldn't attend in person or who had handicaps or disabilities. And, of course, I had several of our photographers on hand to record the event.

The personal shopper and fashion consultants were my idea to add to the fun of the event. I had had the prop department and the merch people actually arrange the sample sale items so they looked nice and mirrored a high-end department store. Usually the sample sale was like one big garage sale with everything piled in boxes for customers to rummage through. I had also curtained off an area of the grand ballroom to act as a makeshift dressing room in case people wanted to try things on. That, too, was new.

After the sample sale to the general public, there was a benefit dinner with an auction for some of the best, most expensive, most exclusive samples that I'd talked the vendors into donating. Samples they'd usually ask for back. Like expensive watches and fine jewelry.

Britt and the merch buyers and I had pulled those earlier and combined them with donated trips and vacation packages to make some really fabulous, enticing things to bid on at dinner. They should bring a good price. As I'd worked on this event, I kept thinking of how much the money would mean to children like Sophia and parents like Vicki.

During dinner, we were putting on a fashion show with items pulled from the sample sale. Diners could bid on the outfits. One of our models for the Doggy and Me line called in sick at the last minute. The poor dog was sick and had to be taken to the vet. I was going to have to step in.

I called Andrea and asked her to pick up Data and bring her to the hotel just before dinner. I'd booked a hotel room for the night for convenience. If necessary, Andrea could stay with Data in my room until she was needed.

And, finally, there was a contest to see which sample sale shoppers could put together the best outfit made up entirely of items from the sale. We took pictures to show during dinner. The dinner audience was going to vote on their favorite. The winner got a hundred-dollar Flashionista gift card.

It was all going to be great fun. As the closer, Justin was supposed to present the hospital with the earnings from the sale. That had been the original plan. I'd sent him an invitation and a reminder. But he hadn't responded. I was prepared to step in.

I dressed casually, but fashionably, for the sale in flat canvas shoes and jeans. All my volunteers were nervous and excited. At the top of the hour, I gave the command. "Let the shopping begin! Open the doors."

Justin

I got my hair cut and dressed in a suit Kay had had hand tailored for me in Milan, along with a custom shirt. Italian suit. Italian shoes. Italian cologne. Italian charisma and charm? That was open for debate.

I took one last look at myself in the mirror, hoping she liked what she saw. Without the beard, I looked like a high school kid again. More like that geeky college guy she remembered. This could backfire on me big time. If Kay didn't like what she saw...

However, Kay deserved to see who she was agreeing to stay with.

This was my gesture. I was giving her what she wanted. If only she would see that I was also giving her my heart.

Kayla

I dressed for dinner and arrived at the banquet hall early so I could supervise the last-minute preparations. The flowers and table settings looked perfect—mums and asters. Bidding paddles for the auction were put out at every table. At last, I was ready to mingle and greet guests.

I'd purchased several tables for key volunteers and staff from Flash, and one for my party—Riggins and a date, Harry and a date, Lazer and his plus-one (to squelch any lingering rumors about us), Britt, who came solo, Dex, also solo, a place for Jus, and me. Our table was right up front in front of the stage and MC podium. The head table, next to a table of hospital dignitaries.

After a decent interval for mingling and networking, and waiting for Jus, I gave the order for dinner to be served. Justin's place remained empty. I kept my chin up. Though that vacant seat was like the proverbial elephant in the room, no one, either at our table or elsewhere, mentioned it. The waiters served our salad. No Jus. They cleared his uneaten salad and served our entrees while the regular auction began. No Jus.

Riggins bid on, and won, a vacation to the Bahamas he didn't need and would probably never take. Britt won a fabulous handbag. Dex didn't see anything to his taste to bid on but promised to make a donation at the end. Lazer outbid a very zealous older lady to win a bracelet for his date, whose name was Amy and seemed very nice.

Dex, who was skinny but had the appetite of five guys twice his size, eyed Justin's steak. So I passed it over without comment. Dex wolfed it down during a ferocious cross-room bidding war on a set of pearl earrings and seven days in Hawaii.

We had a champagne toast without Jus. I got up to help with the fashion show and change into my ensemble. Backstage, I ran into Sophia and Vicki, who were dressed in their matching Mommy and Me clothes. They looked adorable.

I hugged Sophie. "I bet you two get a fabulous bid for your outfits! Who could resist you?"

"Is Justin here?" Sophia's voice was pitched high with childish delight and enthusiasm.

I kneeled to look her in the eye. "Not yet, sweetie. He wasn't sure he'd be able to make it," I lied. "Let's keep our fingers crossed he will."

Sophia pouted. "He *has* to be here! He promised! He's going to bid on my outfit. And win it so I can have it!"

"He did?" I looked at Vicki for confirmation.

"He stopped by a few days ago." She hesitated. "I'm not sure what he promised, or *if* he promised anything."

"He did, Mom!" Sophia got a determined look on her face. "He did! I'm not making it up. He promised."

Vicki gave me a sympathetic look. "See what you're in for? It never stops."

The diners were having fun with the fashion show. Bidding had been wild and enthusiastic. Britt was one of the fashion announcers helping the MC with fashion commentary.

"Next we have Sophia and Vicki modeling a matching mother and daughter ensemble in pink. Sophia is a frequent patient at the hospital and a nurses' favorite. She's wearing..."

Britt continued talking. But I'd stopped listening. The door to the dining room opened and Jus stepped in. My breath caught. His hair was stylishly cut. He was wearing the Italian suit I'd commissioned for him. It fit him like any cliché you can think of and better. He looked hot. And...his face was bare naked. Smooth as a baby's butt, as they say. The beard was gone.

My mouth fell open. From the wings of the stage, I gaped at him. He looked like the old, young Jus, only a hundred times better. A dozen different unnamable emotions swirled through me. This was the man I loved. And yet he reminded me even more of the old, geeky, sweet, college Jus, all grown up and filled out. He certainly filled out his seat in an eye-pleasing way.

My emotions were complex and hard to describe. I only really knew that I wanted him back. And there was a good chance the time for that had passed. He hadn't even wanted to have dinner with his friends and me. Not if I was there.

He winked at Sophia, pulled the pair of colorblind correction glasses I'd given him for his birthday from his pocket, put them on, and grinned.

Sophia had been behaving like a perfect little model up until that point. The moment she saw Jus, she jumped up and down, squealed, took her mother's hand, and pointed to him.

As if on cue, the whole crowd turned to see what the big deal was. A hush fell over the room. Everyone knew who Jus was.

"Sorry I'm late." His grin was infectious. "I don't mean to interrupt. Fifty thousand dollars for the outfits being modeled on stage." He looked around the room, daring anyone to outbid him.

If I knew Jus, he would be happy to bid higher.

The crowd's silence held like they were holding their collective breath. Heads turned. Everyone was waiting for another bidder. Riggins or Lazer could have stepped in. But they didn't. They let Jus have his moment.

"Sold to the stylish gentleman in the back! You have good taste, sir. Someone get that man a paddle so he can bid properly."

Sophia squealed again and jumped off the stage, running to him.

"And your name would be?" the MC said, though he knew full well.

"Justin Green." He scooped Sophia up and hugged her.

The crowd gave a collective "ahh" and erupted in applause.

Data barked in my arms and struggled to get free to go to him. I scratched her behind the ears and held on to her. "Traitor," I whispered to her. "Those two are going to be a hard act to follow."

Yeah, and it wasn't as if I expected Jus to bid on me. I hoped Lazer or Dex would at least do the honors.

Britt glanced at me and made a face. Our secret look of horror we'd used since we were kids. She tried to mouth something to me, but I couldn't understand what she was trying to tell me. I thought it might have been *are you okay?* I nodded just in case.

She cleared her throat, clearly rattled. "Next up we have Mrs. Justin Green and Data modeling matching rhinestone collars and pink ribbons."

I strode on stage like the amateur model I was, hamming it up. Blowing kisses and begging for bids shamelessly. Hey, I was the queen of our sorority on philanthropy day. I knew how to raise money.

Jus went to our table and shook Lazer's hand. He took his seat next to the stage. He set Sophia in my chair. A waiter served her a bowl of ice cream. Someone handed Jus a paddle. It was decidedly down and not in the bidding position.

Britt finished her description. The MC opened the floor for bids. A woman in the back bid first. "That will look adorable on my granddaughter and her puppy."

I was wearing a pink A-line dress that hid my tiny baby bump and pink kitten heels. Sort of a retro sixties look. Data had the rhinestone collar that matched mine and a pink doggy shirt. Which was over the top for a pomsky like Data, who looked more husky than Pomeranian. But still, adorable.

I was trying not to stare at Jus or give myself away by yelling at Dex to bid, for heaven's sake, bid!

Another woman bid. A few more paddles were raised. The bid went up to two hundred dollars.

"Come on! This is for the children, folks! Two-twenty-five, anyone?" The MC looked around the room.

No one moved. Not a paddle stirred.

The MC raised his gavel to close the deal just as Jus raised his.

Jus looked me in the eye. "One million dollars."

I gasped. The diners gasped.

The MC pounded the gavel before Jus could change his mind. "Sold for one million dollars to the gentleman at the head table."

Data barked, squirming to get down. Jus stood, jumped on stage, pulled me into his arms, and kissed me while Data wiggled between us and whined for attention and the audience gave us a standing ovation.

Jus whispered into my ear over the roar of the applause, "You look beautiful in pink. From now on when I tell you you look like a million bucks, you better believe me. Happy mensiversary, baby! I hope they'll be many more." He took off his color correction glasses and put them in his pocket. "I love you. I'd like to try again."

I stroked his bare cheek. It was smooth and soft. "I hope there will be many *anniversaries*. Your cheek's so smooth. What? Did you shave in the lobby?" I had tears in my eyes.

"So?" He gazed into my eyes.

"Soooo? What?" I teased him.

"Can we try again?" His voice broke.

"That's what you really want?" I asked.

He nodded.

I nodded, too. "I love you, too."

He pulled me into his arms and helped me off the stage. I couldn't stop staring at him.

Vicki moved Sophia out of my chair so I could sit. Jus sat next to me, set Data in his lap, and put his arm around me.

After the show, the waiters began serving dessert around the room. A group of them arrived at our table, carrying the mensiversary cake I'd ordered with the bearded cake topper. They were singing, "Happy mensiversary, happy mensiversary!"

When Jus saw the cake topper, his eyes lit up. "Hey! That one actually looks like me. I mean, looked like me." He leaned in and whispered, "We seem to be working at cross purposes." He rubbed his chin and broke out laughing.

"It's symbolic." I laughed. "I think we almost have been all along. But not anymore. Let's not be at cross purposes again."

One of the waiters handed Jus the cake topper and began cutting and serving the cake.

Jus studied it. "This *really* looks like me! Where'd you get it?"

"Like the bearded you." I stroked his cheek again. "I had it specially made."

Dex grabbed it from Jus for a closer look. "Nah. This is much better looking then you ever were." He punched Jus in the arm. "Welcome back to your senses, man."

The Flash volunteers walked in with the cash box from the sale. The MC called Jus to the mic. He got up to present the hospital president with the night's earnings.

"I'd just like to say that tonight wouldn't have been possible without my wife Kayla."

I received a round of applause.

Jus gave a short speech and presented the money.

When he came off the stage, he picked up Data, grabbed my hand, and made our excuses.

He led me by the hand out of the building. Outside the hotel, he suddenly stopped and turned to face me. "Come home. Come home tonight and stay with me forever. I've been a fool. I love you. I want you and the baby. I want our marriage to be real.

"I know I'm asking a lot. We can never be genuinely legally married. We'll have to pretend forever." His voice broke with emotion. "I'd do anything for you, Kay. I *will* do anything. Anything you ask. Anything to make it up to you. We're safe now. In the clear. The ninety days are over. Just come back and be my wife.

Come home, and we can talk all night if we have to to clear the air. Just come home."

"Do you trust me?" I asked, interrupting him.

"Absolutely."

"Okay, then." I smiled at him. "Take me home."

"Really?"

"Yes, stranger. But—"

"Yeah?"

"There's no need to talk all night." I stroked his cheek again. "There are other things I'd really rather spend the night doing."

"Oh, really," he said with a twinkle in his eye. "Like what?"

"Let's just say pregnancy hormones are making me horny."

He took my hand again. "What are we waiting for?"

"If you really can't wait, I have a room here for the night." I laughed. "I just can't get over how different you look. Like you, but like the old you. But not."

He smiled at me.

"Don't worry. I like it. Making love with you tonight is going to be like cheating on you with yourself." I winked at him. "The thought is absolutely thrilling."

"Shut up and come on." He laughed again. "I love you, Kay. Don't ever forget that."

"I know," I said. "I read your letter."

Two Months Later

Justin

I held Kay's hand as the obstetrician spread jelly on Kay's belly and moved the sonogram paddle around.

"What are you hoping for?" the doctor asked as she maneuvered the paddle. "A boy or a girl?"

"A girl," I said. "Like her mother."

Kay shook her head. "I was going to say either."

"As long as it's healthy," we finished together.

The doctor smiled at me. "You're in luck, Mr. Green. I don't see a kickstand. It looks like you're having a girl. And she has all of her arms, and legs, and fingers, and toes."

The doctor turned the screen for me to see. I stared at the 3D image of my baby.

"She looks like her mother." I grinned at Kay. "She's sucking her thumb! Damn, Kay! I think we have another Flashionista on our hands."

Gina Robinson is the award-winning author of the contemporary new adult romances *Rushed, Crushed, Hushed, Reckless Longing, Reckless Secrets,* and *Reckless Together* and the Agent Ex series of humorous romantic suspense novels. She's currently working on the next Jet City Billionaire romance.

Connect with Gina Online:

My Website: http://www.ginarobinson.com/
Twitter: @ginamrobinson
Facebook: www.facebook.com/GinaRobinsonAuthor

www.ingramcontent.com/pod-product-compliance
Lightning Source LLC
Chambersburg PA
CBHW060632130626
46555CB00002B/769